BEST
BONDAGE EROTICA
2014

BEST
BONDAGE
EROTICA
2014

Edited by

RACHEL KRAMER BUSSEL

Foreword by

LAURA ANTONIOU

Published in the United States by Cleis Press, Inc., 2246 Sixth Street, Berkeley, California 94710.

Printed in the United States.
Cover design: Scott Idleman/Blink
Cover photograph: Celesta Danger
Text design: Frank Wiedemann

First Edition.
10 9 8 7 6 5 4 3 2 1

Trade paper ISBN: 978-1-62778-012-4
E-book ISBN: 978-1-62778-025-4

CONTENTS

FOREWORD:
NO BONDAGE PLEASE, I'M KINKY

Here's a secret.

It's a big one, so please, please, don't go telling anyone, but just between you and me and this thing you're holding—printed pages or backlit device—if we could just keep this hush-hush…

I'm not that into bondage.

No, wait, wait, come back, don't just turn the page in annoyance! I know what you're thinking. "What the hell, Laura? This is a book of bondage stories and you want to tell me why it's not hot? I already think it's hot, that's why I got the book!"

You think I'm insulting your taste. I get it. But really—stick with me a moment.

Bondage is the most basic building block of kinky sex, isn't it? Ask any random (consenting adult) person on the street what kinky sex is, and they'll conjure up images of someone tied to a bed, maybe blindfolded, while someone else waves a riding crop around or intones dire threats concerning recent naughty behavior. It's the very definition of Kink, the *B* in BDSM, the edgy sex act most likely to wind up illustrating an article on spicing up your sex life.

But it's much more than that. The sensuous feel of soft fabric as it winds along your forearm, the sturdy security of a stiff leather band buckled around an ankle, the icy rigidity of steel around your throat. These aren't just tools, toys or tokens.

These are signifiers.

Just look at the array of constricting tales before you—from hesitant experimentation to the long-plotted capture of an erotic trophy. Sinuous rope-play contrasts with a struggle between the human body and...a really tight jacket.

No, not that kind. But my point is, the bondage isn't just a method, it isn't just a kink—it is a definer of power, time and space, teasing ecstasy and agony. Here you have taunting, withholding tops, dominant and sneering in their superior position of freedom. But over there is the careful artist weaving a performance of pleasure, an act of worship or service cleverly disguised as control. The privacy of a bedroom or the empty, echoing hallways of a workplace are backdrops to a theater of captivity and torment or romance with a side order of discipline.

And yet, I tell you, I am not that into it. It's a shameful secret, really. Because it's so basic, so vital, so important, people travel all over the world to learn the secrets of bondage, whether they look to the Western cowboy styles or the Far East for Japanese techniques. They spend hours designing and testing restraints for the most wily escape artist and the most delicate of carpal-tunnel-endangered wrists. Build a better mousetrap and the world will beat down your door? Build a better chastity device and they'll come charging with credit cards in hand.

But you see, amid all my kinks, the supreme one for me is that of authority and obedience. So in my twisted, delightful fantasies, telling someone to hold still is all the bondage one should need. Or, as I like to joke, I use bondage just to make sure they won't run away when I hit them. Or worse. Cue rim shot!

And yet, I was delighted to read this collection—and many, many other stories containing physical bondage. And not just because I am a person of many tastes in reading.

You see, even though you won't find high-tech bondage equipment in my closet (no room) or a manual on how to tie some knot I can't pronounce on my shelves, I do love—and value—one vital aspect of restraint. And that's the freedom it entails.

Yes, freedom. The freedom to let everything *go* and just know there is no way to escape the dastardly plans of the villainous noble/spy/kidnapper/inquisitor/masked intruder. The freedom to stand apart from my loves and whisper from behind them, and keep them in suspense until I am good and ready. The sheer luxury of relaxing into the velvet padding or straining against the suede straps and allowing the pure emotions and drives to come out to play.

This is why so many of the stories have a fantasy flavor to them, whether acknowledged or not. Sure, some of the characters will break out of their hot bondage-fueled beatings and sex, kiss and shower and head back to mundane lives and you will read exactly that. But in others, the question hovers...was this real? Or a pure fantasy? Would someone really want that, do that? Did they? Ever? Really?

Should you?

And in between all the careful, loving partners checking in with each other, issuing safewords and kisses of reassurance, there are the harder edges that dance on precipices like coercion and humiliation, threats of abandonment or debauchery and maybe those stories sound less real, and yet...

They are made possible because of the bondage. Because...

what could you do? What could anyone do, if he or she were helplessly tied up, secured to that infernal device?

That's the freedom bondage offers. And you will find it here. Freedom to enjoy the romance of longtime lovers familiar with their drives and desires, or newfound playmates negotiating surrender and force in a dance of seduction. In privacy or with an audience, even virtual bondage gets a turn in this something-for-everyone tasting menu of all things constricting.

So, don't pity me, because I only know two knots and one of them laces my sneakers and the other arranges my necktie. Just enjoy the delicious freedom of restraint offered in this book and indulge yourself in some vicarious pleasure, as I did.

What you do next is entirely up to you. Unless someone ties you down first.

Laura Antoniou

INTRODUCTION:
CRUEL TO BE KIND, AND VICE VERSA

One of the joys of editing erotic anthologies is marveling at the diversity of the authors' imaginations. While this is my fourth year editing the *Best Bondage Erotica* series, it's always a surprise to me when I start reading stories and seeing just how many ways someone can be tied up, strung up or otherwise restrained.

What you'll read in *Best Bondage Erotica 2014* isn't a how-to manual, but rather a taste of twenty hot bondage tales that don't skimp on the sadism, masochism or sexiness of the encounters. These writers show and tell exactly what it means to wield the special power of being in charge of someone else. In "Pegged," Emily Bingham writes, "It's his turn to be small and defenseless for an evening. I want to be so kind to him that it becomes cruel." Sometimes pop culture portrays kinksters and bondage fans as all cruel, without a shred of kindness. The dirty little secret is that these characters are, in fact, both; they manipulate rope, handcuffs, leather straps, a St. Andrew's cross, a chair, and, in Raziel Moore's "My Own Device," a special contraption crafted just for bondage, with the ultimate aim of pleasing their partners—when they're done having their fun, teasing them, hurting them, screwing them and generally making them writhe, squirm and indulge in the delight of helplessness.

I'm delighted to present this latest edition of *Best Bondage Erotica*, which I hope will delight those who know exactly what it feels like to be at someone else's mercy (or have someone else at your mercy) as well as those who simply want to picture the joys of being bound in vivid, elaborate, beautiful, cruel and kind detail.

Rachel Kramer Bussel
New York City

ROPE DANCER

Kathleen Tudor

Emily was gorgeous, of course, but when it comes to the performing arts, gorgeous girls are a dime a dozen. It was the rope that truly drew my attention, and her beauty only ensured that the hook was well and truly set.

The circus show was a publicity ploy at my favorite local bar, and I decided to pay the fifteen dollars for a ticket to sit in on it since they were crowding out my Friday night watering hole, anyway. The clown, who also served as prop master and rigger, was amusing, mostly because his actual job was so transparent; the belly dancers were a tad on the old side and out of shape and the hula hooper was great until she accidentally sent one of her hoops flying into the crowd like a *chakram*.

There was no question—the real gem of the night was Emily.

By the time her finale was announced, I was tired and torn between pity and irritation at the crowd, the noise and the amateur show. Emily stepped out from the curtained-off "back-stage" area, let one hand slide up the thick rope in the center of the room and threw her head back, falling still for the seconds until the music started. Then she levitated.

I know she didn't really levitate, but that's how it seemed. Her other hand joined the first on the rope, and then she slowly floated upward until she was hanging upside down. I was impressed, but not caught. Not until she started to wrap her body around the rope and the rope around her body.

The way she moved was like magic in the air, steady and graceful, never hurried, with a serene look of peace on her face. I forgot all of my irritation and my warm beer, and focused on the way that thick rope slid over her skin, into and out of poses that showed off her flexibility and strength. She used the rope like it was another part of her body, always highlighting the beauty and never awkward, out of place or in the way.

She glided from upside down to right side up, and I stared at the way the colored lights made her blonde curls glisten green and red and blue. When she performed a dramatic drop, falling several feet before catching herself on a clever knot, my heart jumped into my throat.

And then she would shift, twist her body, reach up for the rope, and those clever knots would fall away, the rope hanging straight and true, waiting for her next cunning wrap or daring drop. It terrified me, those knots-that-were-not-knots, the way that they could hold her plummeting body in one moment, and then fall away to nothing in the next.

When she turned upside down at the very top, hooking one leg, passing the rope behind her, and sliding slowly to the ground, it took me a long moment to realize that the fact that she was now resting flat on her back on the floor meant that the show was over.

I exploded to my feet with applause, as did most of the other patrons of the bar, and clapped even as I glared when the rest of the cast came out to share in the glory. The show had been carried by that little golden girl with the bouncing curls. I had to meet her.

Fortunately, the bar had no real stage, and although the cast had curtained off that small area in which to change, rest, and store their tools, there was no back way for her to modestly escape through. I asked Jolie, the bartender, if the girl had a regular order, then took the Long Island and a fresh beer for myself back to my table to wait.

When I finally saw her, she'd thrown on a pair of jeans and a T-shirt that showed off her flat belly. She stopped to talk to someone, shifting until her back was to me, so I came up behind her and waited for the other person to move off. Then I reached around to hold the drink out in front of her, and whispered in her ear, "You carried that show."

She jumped and turned to face me, and I held the drink up for her again. "Long Island? Jolie said you like them."

She took it, wary, and murmured a polite thank-you, though I didn't know whether she meant for the compliment or for the drink. I watched her eyes roam behind me, looking for her avenue of escape, and I knew I was losing her before I'd even caught her. It was time to go big.

"So, do you like all kinds of ropes, or just the kind you can hang from?"

That caught her attention. She looked startled as her eyes snapped back to me. "Pardon?"

"I was just wondering if you like the feel of ropes on your skin when you're not the one in control." I suddenly felt like a world-class idiot. She looked me up and down, buying herself time, I thought. I straightened, feeling foolish and wanting to gather my pride around me, but something in her eyes had changed.

"Maybe you should show me what you mean," she said.

I laughed. "Have a drink. Decide if you even like me first. Are you from around here?"

I guided her to an empty table and she sat, waiting to make eye contact with Jolie and get a nod before she took a sip of the drink I'd brought her. I decided I liked that about her.

"Yeah, I moved here two years ago. The circus community is pretty good in this area, you know? Welcoming. Good for new performers who aren't up to the big circus standards yet."

"You seemed pretty damn good to me. A lot better than the rest of the troupe."

She thanked me in a way that made it clear I'd made her uncomfortable. "I've been performing little gigs like this since just before I moved here, but I haven't really been able to land anything bigger. Some people are just better at marketing themselves, I guess. You?"

"Live here? Yeah. I've got an apartment a couple blocks thataway." I gestured with my beer, and she followed my hand with her eyes.

"Where you also like to play with rope?" she asked quietly.

"Well, I can't say I've ever tied *myself* up." I grinned. "I'm a fair hand with a knot, though."

"Walking distance?"

"I'll even carry your books."

She didn't have any books, but she did let me carry the heavy gym bag that held her rope and her costume. "I'm surprised you don't snap in half under this weight," I teased, but she turned to me and flexed sassily, and the muscles of her arms popped into definition, reminding me of the way she'd casually suspended, lifted and pulled her own body weight for a five-minute show. "Wow. That is insanely sexy."

"Need some help carrying the big, heavy bag, you poor, weak little lady?" she teased back.

"Come to think of it, you could probably kick my ass handily. Fortunately for me, you seem keen on letting me tie you up and render you harmless."

She laughed at that, and I led her up the steps to my apartment, gesturing to let her go first. I put the bag down with relief—the damn thing was actually really heavy—and casually shook out my burning shoulder before she could turn around and see.

"So what next?" she asked, turning slowly to take in my apartment.

"That depends. How much do you want to play? I could just tie you up and let you go again, if you want, or I could tie you up and cut your clothes off of you." She glared at me. "Or we could start naked and I could tie you up and have my way with you."

"This was a remarkably stupid thing to do, wasn't it?"

"Follow a stranger home and let her tie you up? Yeah, generally. I promise not to do anything you don't want me to, but so would the creeps and serial killers." I smiled gently, and got out from between her and the door. "If you want to leave, I understand. It'd be nice if I could get your number first, though."

She looked at me, then the door, then at the door behind her that led into the bedroom. "This may surprise you," she said, "but I'm sort of an adrenaline junkie." She backed toward the bedroom, and my mouth went dry with desire as I followed slowly after her. She waited until she'd cleared the doorway before she hooked her fingers under the tight little baby tee and started to pull it up. "Let's go with naked."

She drew me like iron filings to a magnet. "I'm good with that."

She wiggled her hips teasingly before she pulled her jeans

down to stand before me in just a pair of panties and her lacy bra. I smiled encouragingly, trying not to drool, and moved past her to sit on the bed. She did one slow spin for me in her lingerie, then reached back and unhooked her bra to let it fall away. Tempting as it was, I resisted the urge to move toward her, waiting patiently as she displayed her breasts for me, touching and playing with them. My time would come...

I couldn't do anything about the small moan that escaped me when she finally bent down to slip her panties off her slim hips, down her long legs and off. She flashed a smile at me, and then lifted one leg in front of her, grabbed her foot and straightened her leg up over her head. "Shall I strike a pose?"

"Not unless you intend to hold it for the next hour or so." I'd never tied up someone this flexible before, and I quickly reviewed my repertoire and discarded a few bonds that were only effective because of the limits on normal human bendiness. I also had to discard the vivid mental images of what some of those poses from her show would look like while she was naked and in my bed.

"I'd like to start with an arm binding," I told her, standing and moving to my rope cabinet. I pulled out a length of soft cotton dyed a rich red. "Upper arm to upper arm, then all the way down to your wrists." The speed of her breath picked up, and I moved with intentional slowness, savoring the way the thought of being bound seemed to arouse her. "Have you been tied up before?" I slid the rope around one upper arm to start the binding, and she shivered as it slid over her skin.

"No, but I've thought about it," she said. Her voice had dropped to something husky and rough, and I took a deep breath to restore my patience. I was much too close, and got a whiff of floral shampoo, instead. It sent my pulse into overdrive, and I clenched my teeth and forced my hands to move slowly and surely as I pulled her arms back and together. They got disconcertingly close together before I reached the limits of her flexibility. Cool.

"Sometimes struggling is part of the game, so instead of saying 'no' or 'stop,' we use something called a safeword. Lots of people use the word 'red.' It means that all play instantly stops, and we resolve whatever the problem is." I pulled the rope through a loop and passed it around her arm. It made me smile to feel Emily shuddering beneath my fingers every time the rope hissed over her skin. "You should definitely use it if you feel like any part of you is getting cold or numb, because we want to keep your circulation going. Okay?"

"I understand," she said. I had reached her wrists, and I finished the knots off out of reach, then tied the extra into a little bow between her hands as a pretty finishing touch.

"How does that feel?"

"I can't move," she said, shrugging her shoulders to test the bonds and wiggling her upper body. Her slender form moved enticingly, and I purred approval. "It's amazing." Her voice had taken on a tone of wonder, and she turned to face me. "I'm helpless, but I feel so...free."

I brushed my hand over her face, and she leaned into my touch. "That's because you're counting on me to take care of you." I let my hand move lower, caressing the skin of her neck, tracing her collarbone, then drawing one finger around the curve of her breast. It was delightfully full and soft, and her pink nipple drew into an even sharper peak as I got close. "You've surrendered control, and there's freedom in that. All you have to do is *be*. It's my responsibility now to make sure that everything is okay, and that we both come away from this experience happy."

Her eyes had drifted shut and her breasts lifted and fell in a quick rhythm that spoke to me of arousal and excitement. Some people put up with being tied because their partner likes it, or because it's a means to an end. Emily was my favorite kind—the rope itself was enough to send her into subspace with boiling blood and a heated body. It was all about the bondage, the feel of rope over skin, the way it captured and caressed at the same time. I smiled in delight as I guided her toward the bed.

"Are you comfortable kneeling? I'd like to bind your legs, too."

Emily's breath hitched, and she moved quickly into position, leaning into my helping hands as if this were a long-established routine. It made my heartbeat stutter to see the way that she responded to my every guiding touch. Was there ever anything hotter than a beautiful, powerful woman putting herself trustingly into my hands?

The first short pieces of rope went around her ankles, one each, and I left long tails to dangle. I knew she would be excited with just the feel of the rope against her skin, even if it wasn't actually binding her into position yet. Then I started to weave, tying her ankles to her upper thighs to fix her in that kneeling position, passing the rope back and forth through that tight fold of flesh between calf and thigh perhaps one more time than I had to, just to watch her shudder with pleasure as the rope surged over her skin.

And then, of course, I had to do the second leg to match. She looked like a goddess or maybe a sacrifice, trussed up in dark jewel red with her arms going straight down her back and her breasts jutting forward. It tempted me toward a breast tie, too.

"You are so beautiful like that," I told her, running a finger along her skin just above the arm binding. I reached down and touched her hands to make sure they weren't going cold and bloodless, then moved to her front, licked one jutting nipple and blew cool air across it. She writhed with pleasure, but couldn't get far with the knots holding her fast. It made me moan to see her so helpless and sexy and trusting. "I have a Polaroid camera," I said. "I'd love to take a picture of you. Just one, and you can keep it. I just think something this amazing should be recorded, even if it doesn't last."

"Yes," she said. "Take it." Her voice was thin and breathy with arousal, and I moved closer, grabbed her by the hair and leaned over her, tipping her head back as I kissed her senseless. Her body was hot and soft as it pressed against me, and I let my other hand wander up and down her arm. The sensation she would feel would be one of intermittent touch as my fingers wandered from rope to flesh to rope again; it would remind her vividly of the way she was bound—as if she was likely to forget.

When I pulled away, she gasped for more and I had to steady her before I could grab my camera and snap the shot. It was perfect, the way she stared hungrily at me behind the lens. I pulled the picture free and set it down with her clothing so she would remember it later.

"Part of me wants to just keep tying, but I think you look like you're ready for some more play," I told her, a note of smug teasing in my voice. She whimpered as I moved to stand next to her. I'd positioned her sideways near the edge of the bed so that she was in the perfect position to touch and tease from a standing position. I kissed her more lightly this time, and let my hand play over the front of her body as I traveled steadily toward her hot center.

I could already smell her arousal, so it was no surprise to dip my fingers into her folds and find them saturated and swollen with her desire. I let just the tips of my fingers slide between her lips and brought them up to my own mouth to taste her. She let out a sweet sigh of desire as I licked my fingers clean. "Do you want some, too?" I asked. I ran one finger through the wetness and brought it up to her mouth. She sucked my finger into her mouth with surprising alacrity for someone so deep in subspace, licking and flicking her tongue over it as I slowly fucked her mouth.

"I love how responsive you are," I told her, and finally took custody of my finger back. I traced my tongue over her lips, staying just out of reach, and she whimpered with frustration when she realized that she couldn't rise up on her legs to force the kiss. I laughed softly before I gave in, pressing my lips against her soft mouth and sliding my fingers deep into her cunt at the same time.

Emily writhed against me as I penetrated her with fingers and tongue, taking possession of her body through sheer force of presence. Our tongues danced together as I plundered her mouth. Her body writhed and rolled as much as she could make it while my fingers slid deep inside her. She was sensitive and open beneath me, and I ran my free hand through her hair, nearly as tense with desire and excitement as she was.

Her intermittent whimpers turned into one long moan of desire before I shifted my hand and gave her what she needed. I moved my thumb to massage her clit even as I curled my fingers and found that spongy bit of flesh that marked her G-spot. Some women hardly feel a thing, but Emily cried out into my mouth and her whole body tightened and shook as her pussy clamped around my fingers in undulating waves of orgasm. I smiled as I devoured her cries, and curled and uncurled my fingers, drawing out her orgasm and sending her cries higher and higher until it was impossible to keep my mouth closed over hers.

I moved to her throat, instead, kissing and licking and nibbling the sensitive flesh there as she threw back her head and screamed. When she started to giggle and thrash, I pulled my hand gently free and smeared her cream across her beautiful breasts before taking first one, then the other, into my mouth and licking it away. They rose and fell impressively as she struggled to catch her breath. I found one of her nipples and bit down gently, and she mewed softly.

They were perfect breasts, large enough to bounce and sway but not yet affected by the steady pull of gravity. What else could be expected from someone who spent her free time defying gravity every day? I tasted the creamy skin and sucked the rosy nipples into my mouth, tonguing them diligently and lifting the full weight of her breasts in my hands. I could be a lesbian *just* for the breasts and the way that they feel when you lift them and cup them and gently squeeze.

Emily arched into my touch, and I expanded the tease, running my fingers up and down her sides and belly in swirling patterns to send goose bumps trailing in my wake. "Want more," she gasped, and I smiled and nipped at her breast one last time.

"Me, too." I hurried out of my clothes and tossed them aside, not caring where anything landed. Then I climbed up onto the bed, straddled one of Emily's bound thighs and leaned over her, supporting my body weight and hers as I bent her back until I could press my pussy into the flesh and rope across the top of her leg. With one hand braced on the bed and the other one around her back to support her weight, I began to rock my hips, rubbing my clit against her.

It would have been easy to get off just feeling myself slide against the firm flesh of her thighs, but with the ropes crisscrossing her skin, my clit was assaulted with sensation. I tried to focus on kissing the soft white expanse of her neck and collarbone, but my orgasm crashed over me so quickly that it stole my breath and shook my entire body. She cried out with me, echoing my pleasure, and I pulled her forward and over, onto me, before I went completely limp.

It took a few minutes of regrouping before I had the energy to ask her how her arms and legs felt. "My toes are tingling, but it could just be from those kisses," she said.

"I should untie you." And though she whimpered a complaint, she sat patiently as I eased each knot free and pulled the ropes across her sensitive skin and away. When she was completely free, I sat down next to her and took her feet in my hands, massaging them gently, both for pleasure and to help her keep her circulation up. Then just to feel her strong hands in mine, I took her warm fingers and did the same.

"What comes next?" she asked, tracing the rope indentations across her thighs with something like lust in her eyes.

"That's still up to you, my pretty little rope dancer," I teased, bringing the hand I had been massaging to my face and letting her thread her fingers through my hair. "You can go if you want to, but it would be nice if you'd like to stay longer."

She smiled and used her hand in my hair to pull me closer, sitting up so that we could press our breasts together and hold each other close as we kissed. She scratched at my back and pulled at my hair until I rolled, pulling her with me so that I was lying on my back while she straddled my lap. When her little fingers danced over my nipples, I thought that sometimes it's worth it to skip the rope and leave hands free. And then her fingers moved lower, and it was the last thing I thought for a long time.

She was gone when I woke up the next morning, in a sex-mussed bed, feeling deliciously sore all over. She'd taken her clothes and her bag, but she'd left the Polaroid on the kitchen table, a phone number written across the bottom with a firm, feminine hand. I smiled as I went to make coffee.

That was a year ago, and I still love to see Emily in ropes, whether my own or hers, high in the air. And I still have that little Polaroid displayed on my bedroom mirror where I can see her bound form and her tousled hair and lustful, hungry eyes waiting to devour me each morning as I dress.

BEHIND THE DOOR

Kay Jaybee

The first van drew up at exactly half past twelve. It was never late.

Nina could feel the beat of her pulse accelerate as she watched from her office window.

Every day the same van came. It was white with gaudy adverts proclaiming the painting trade of its driver emblazoned along its sides.

Pretending to adjust the blinds, Nina found herself holding her breath as the spiky-haired, stocky man, with paint-daubed shorts and grubby T-shirt, left his vehicle and dashed through the door to the empty shop opposite.

Tearing her eyes away, Nina checked her watch. In three minutes it would be twelve thirty-five, and the next van would arrive.

This van was blue, and much larger, with a ladder strapped to the roof, and claims of being able to improve your double-glazing written on the hood. This driver was taller than the first, his ginger hair cropped closely to the outline of his skull.

He, too, all but ran into the neglected shop.

It had been a bookshop once. Popular, busy and friendly. Then one day a year ago, it was suddenly deserted, as if the Internet revolution had ruined it within the space of a day. Now it sat, with a single curtain, faded and worn, pulled across the length of the old shop window, blocking the outside world from whatever, or whoever, waited inside.

Conscious that she hadn't typed a word into her computer for at least five minutes, Nina turned to her keyboard and filled in a few more blanks on the spreadsheet before her. She had another three minutes before the final vehicle came at twelve forty.

They were rarely early, and they were never ever late.

The red car, a hatchback bursting with the tools of the carpentry trade, pulled up next to the blue van. Its tall, slim owner, whose shaved head was always covered with a baseball cap as he went in—but always bare when he came out—checked the time before he strode with purpose toward the solid wooden door.

The door used to be propped open with a solid-iron cat-shaped doorstop all day, but now it was left firmly closed. Prying eyes were prevented from even glimpsing within, as the men never opened it beyond the requirements of their own body size as they sidled inside.

"Are you coming for lunch?" The question from Laura, her only colleague in the small accounts office, made Nina jump as she continued to pretend to work, while keeping an eye on the activities outside.

"Better work through today, sorry, I'm a bit behind."

"Again?" Her friend smiled at her. "Too much daydreaming out the window, honey! I'll bring you back a latte."

Wishing Laura would hurry up and disappear, Nina smiled back at her. "Thanks. That would be lovely."

Relieved to finally be alone, Nina stopped tapping blindly on her keyboard and devoted all of her attention to the shop opposite. Every day she mulled over a whole host of possibilities as to what they were doing in there. At first she had taken very little notice, assuming that they were about to do up the premises to ready them for a new owner. But as the weeks had turned into months, and nothing seemed to have happened to the property, yet the men still appeared every day, Nina's imagination became more lurid.

The bookshop had belonged to a striking redheaded woman called Louisa, whose age would be impossible to gauge. One day she'd been there, the next she was gone. Nina, who'd been a regular customer in her bookshop, frequently had the impression that Louisa wouldn't be someone you'd want to argue with. Always immaculate, always calm, her voice had been strong and positive, giving off the vibe that arguing with her would be more than a little unwise. Not that Nina had ever had reason to disagree with the woman. Her book recommendations had always been excellent, and her welcome warm.

Was she still in there? Was it Louisa, the slightly domineering proprietor with an interesting array of boots and chunky jewelry, whom the three men went to visit each lunchtime?

Nina knew she was becoming obsessed. Each evening at home her musings became more exotic, as, with her hand between her legs, her speculations wild, she pictured the redhead ordering each of the tradesmen to their knees the instant they walked through her front door.

Curled in her bed, strumming the folds of her pussy, Nina would clearly visualize Louisa standing in the center of the forgotten shop. Instead of books upon the shelves, there would be the tools of her new trade—whips, handcuffs and dildos set alongside rows of ropes and butt plugs, nipple clamps and vibrators. Any sex toy Nina could conjure in her mind would be lying on those wooden shelves, each patiently waiting for the hour when the men came.

Cloaked in velvet, a hood over her long, loose, curled hair, Louisa would wear nothing but knee-length scarlet boots, the pair with a zip running right up the back that Nina had admired and secretly coveted so often. Around her neck she'd wear a thick-cut, blood-red, heart-shaped pendant, its dazzling brightness highlighting how very pale her naked flesh was as she paced the room, awaiting her servants' arrival.

Shaking herself, aware of a sweet dampness spreading between her legs as she indulged in erotic speculation, Nina directed her eyes back to the computer terminal before her. There was no point staring at the shop door. Nothing would happen for an hour; then, at five-minute intervals, the men would reappear. The owner of the white van would leave first, followed by his blue-van-driving colleague and finally the carpenter.

It was their carefully staggered arrivals and departures that fascinated Nina as much as what might happen while they were inside the shop. Her knowledge of sex wasn't vast, but she knew that in five minutes you could achieve a hell of a lot. Men certainly didn't need that long to become naked and aroused. Sixty seconds would probably sort those jobs out.

Trying to ignore how tight her breasts felt beneath her bra, Nina toyed with the idea of creeping down to the shop and trying to peer into the window or listen at the keyhole. She didn't quite dare though. The images of what they might do to her if she was discovered sent trickles of fearful arousal through her, as she temporarily abandoned all hope of work, and let her brain fill in the gaps.

At that moment Nina was sure that all three men would be kneeling before Louisa. They would all be attired in the same way. Tight blue-denim shorts, cut marginally too small so that their cocks had no room to maneuver beneath them, would encase their lower halves. They would be allowed no underwear, their commando status causing maximum discomfort and arousal to their imprisoned shafts.

Their torsos—muscular and hard from manual labor—would be bare, as would their lower legs and feet. That was what had taken the time; the five-minute intervals as the men arrived would be spent in a ritual of undressing and putting on the shorts. Their mistress stood directly before them, arms crossed, watching each move critically through her catlike eyes, allowing them to remove their garments one piece at a time at the speed she set, and only on her command. Only once each individual male was ready would they be allowed to sit on the hard shop floor and wait for the action of the hour to begin.

Unable to imagine Louisa without a book to hand, Nina visualized her holding a notebook out before her, in which she kept a record of the men's previous performances. If they'd behaved well and pleased her, they would receive better treatment on their next visit. Poor behavior, or failure to conform to the high standards she set, would mean punishment or physical neglect.

Nina, her eyes closed, safe in the knowledge that Laura would be out for at least another forty minutes, pictured the white van driver. His face was grave as Louisa read out her displeasure, tapping her black pen on top of her notebook as if to punctuate every word of her annoyance. He had failed to make her climax the day before, so today his own satisfaction would be hampered by the presence of handcuffs. After swift and unflinching orders, his ginger counterpart did his mistress's bidding, and snapped a pair of cold metal handcuffs around white-van man's wrists, yanking his arms roughly behind his back while he knelt, cowering on the dusty wooden floor.

The moment his companion was shackled, the ginger man retook his position in the queue of three before Louisa, as she walked up and down before them. In her silence, the gloom of the unlit room enveloped the dominatrix like warm fog, out of which she shone like an enticing beacon of temptation.

Louisa inclined her head toward the men, as if giving them a signal to begin. They rose together, the tethered man clumsy but still forthcoming, as their mistress lay back on the only item of furniture in the discarded shop, a faded red-velvet chaise lounge, which Nina remembered perching on as she flicked through various books.

Nina's eyes reopened. The image in her mind was so clear, so real. She hadn't been aware that her right hand had snaked its way up inside her white blouse, so immersed was she in her thoughts. Her gaze refocused on the curtained window on the street opposite, wondering whether, if she stared hard enough, she would miraculously develop X-ray vision and see precisely what they were really up to within.

Keeping her wide blue eyes fixed on the door, Nina allowed her fingertips to brush the tips of her nipples, and gave her kinky thoughts free reign.

The cloak had fallen back, so only the hood remained over Louisa's silky hair. The velvet fabric's edges draped on the floor, her exposed pearl flesh showed the red heart pendant nestled in the very center of her cleavage.

As she lay, her hands limp at her sides, she remained very much in control, a pagan queen awaiting the service of her loyal followers. A wave of her hand, and the two unfettered servants divested themselves of their denim, their cocks stiff, hard and as ready for action as any Nina had ever seen.

The ginger-haired man, who appeared to be the favored slave, rose from his knees and, with a double check toward his mistress, collected a vial of oil from the nearest shelf. Unstoppering the small, conical-shaped bottle, he gestured to his shaved companion, who strode to the opposite side of the recliner. Finally, the handcuffed man came, his position obviously lowly, hovering at the booted feet, only able to observe, his dick aching within his shorts, resigning himself to receiving no satisfaction that day.

"Begin." Louisa's voice was deep and sensual, without a trace of uncertainty. There was no visible tensing of her body as the oil vial was held directly above the red pendant, and tipped.

Unconsciously, Nina held her breath as she observed the pictures in her mind.

The oil, thick and gloopy, seemed to travel in slow motion toward the line that divided Louisa's magnificent chest. A heavy scent of sandalwood filled the air as the first droplet hit the brilliant red of the heart stone, and then trickled onward, running between her breasts. That first droplet was swiftly followed by a second, and then a third, each landing precisely on the spot of the first, a monument to the steadiness of the slave's hands.

Corking the bottle once more, the ginger man placed it back on the shelf before he and the shaved slave—with a patience that should have won him an award—began to work the oil deep into the tits before them.

Nina wondered how badly they wanted to speed up, to hurriedly push the oil into her flesh, rather than sedately rub it. How much they wanted to rush, to lean forward and take the scarlet nipples between their teeth, to plant their shafts between the thighs of the languid creature reclined before them.

Was their keeper struggling not to beg her men to go faster? Maybe Louisa wasn't so controlled as her calm countenance would have them believe.

As the oil was simultaneously caressed into each breast, Nina could almost feel the fingertips of the men against her own chest. The slippery warm sensation of the sensual massage was reflected in the slickening of her pussy, and Nina thought, Louisa's pussy, as well.

Was the scent of sex, rich and heady, being overpowered by the aroma of oil, or did the heavy atmosphere of eroticism merely cancel it out?

Nina's fingers worked harder on her own tips, the presence of her satin kickers becoming more and more obvious between her thighs. She hardly dared blink. Just in case today was the day the door opened early. Just in case it was opened wide enough for her aerial view to give her the briefest glimpse of what lay inside.

There was no movement. Nina looked at her clock. There was still twenty minutes before they were due to leave in reverse order to their arrival. Reverting to her ponderings, Nina could only conclude that the oil anointment of her imaginings was still going on.

Once every drip of the liquid had been soaked into her breasts, Louisa issued a further signal. This was, after all, a ceremony for her enjoyment and not for the men around her. Lifting the pendant's stone, after careful consideration, she pointed it toward the men in order. The first to have the heart favored in their direction would receive the most gratification; the second would receive some, while the third man would merely be a thing to provide enjoyment for his mistress.

Nina fidgeted slightly in her swivel chair. Her panties were uncomfortable, her channel felt painfully empty and her chest felt as though it was being held hostage within the confines of her bra.

The ginger man would be astride Louisa by now, his beautiful cock consumed deep within her throat. Low animal mewls of pleasure would escape from the corners of the mistress's mouth as the shaved man, his hands everywhere, would attach his mouth to each of her tits in turn, lapping the oil, savoring the almost bitter taste against the exquisite flavor of her luscious skin.

Meanwhile, the third man, still a prisoner within his shorts, his dick pushing painfully against the rough fabric, had lowered himself to his knees. Unable to touch Louisa with his hands, his tongue would worship at her pussy, lapping away the gush of liquid as this part of the mistress failed to hide how aroused she was.

A light perspiration had bloomed on Nina's palms, a perspiration that mingled with the liquid from her own channel as she played her nub between her fingers. She knew this fantasy—one of thousands about life behind the door that kept her masturbating night after night—had to stop. She couldn't concentrate at work all morning waiting for lunchtime, and she couldn't do anything after lunch as she was too aroused to focus. Enough was enough. She had to know. She had to know now.

Nina hadn't realized what she was doing until she was already down the stairs, and her hand was pushing open the door to the block of offices where she worked. As she crossed the road, a voice at the back of her head began to shout. *Do I really want to know?* If the four of them were just discussing a new shop fitting, or having a crafty smoke of some dodgy substance or other, her disappointment would be crippling.

As her hand reached for the door, the same wooden door she had stared at every lunchtime for weeks and weeks, her heart drummed harder in her chest, and her throat dried. *I have to know!* Nina pushed at the door. It was locked. Vaguely aware she was acting like a deranged stalker, she lifted the letterbox, ready to peep inside. It had been blocked up on the inside.

Walking alongside the window, she tried to squint between a

tiny gap in the curtain, but it was too small, and the lack of light inside confirmed her imagination's assumption that, whatever happened behind the door, happened in the semidark.

A sudden scrape of metal made her jump, pulling Nina abruptly to her senses as she realized what she was doing. A prickle of panic shot down her spine. What if they'd spotted her? She'd wanted to see but not be seen! There was probably nothing to see anyway.

She was halfway back across the road when an arm reached out and caught her elbow. Nina spun around, ready to push her assailant away.

She froze as her eyes fell on the blood-red pendant around the woman's neck.

Louisa smiled into Nina's eyes, her gaze both welcome but also warning her. "Your curiosity has been noted."

Nina's mouth opened and closed, but no words came out.

"Would you like to see?" Louisa was steering Nina back toward the shop, her low-cut, ankle-length scarlet dress brushing against the ground as she walked.

"I'm really sorry, I was just daydreaming, I didn't mean to..." Nina's words died on her lips as her sex contracted and her stomach did a backflip.

There was no chaise lounge in the shop. The deserted room didn't smell of sandalwood. It didn't need to. It just smelt of sex—raw, uncomplicated, desperately desired sex, the source of which was the three tradesmen. They were not wearing shorts. They were not wearing anything. They were, however, ready, waiting and fastened together with a circle of rope, as if they had all been kidnapped by a cartoon character.

"I'm sorry my boys can't come to greet you properly. A little rude of them, I admit, but as you can see, they are a little tied up at the moment..." Louisa studied Nina intently as she spoke, the lust radiating from her feline eyes difficult to disguise.

"So, Nina, I am sure you have a million questions, but the whys and wherefores of how this state of affairs came about can wait. They are very dull anyway. Instead, let me explain what is happening right now; what happens here, at this hour, every day. This is sex roulette. Each day my boys are tied together in a back-to-back-style triangle. One of them is chosen by the roll of these three poker chips..." She lifted up three plastic discs, each colored according to the bodywork color of the vehicle the men owned. "But as there is only one of me, only one of them gets what he came for; until the next day, when they have the chance to get lucky all over again."

Louisa cupped the chin of the ginger-haired man as she spoke, his erection as solid as his colleagues', their legs all showing the marks of recent whippings. Nina suspected that whatever she had imagined happening behind the door, it was nothing compared to what actually went on.

The mistress clasped her free hand firmly around Nina's and walked her, nerves racing, toward her willing hostages. "Today, my darling boys, it looks as if the odds have just doubled...."

MY OWN DEVICE

Raziel Moore

We are all prisoners
of our own device
but my device
has room for you.
(Inspired by The Eagles' "Hotel California")

"Show me," she said, the faintest trace of huskiness in her voice.

Though I'd been planning this since soon after my last visit with Anna three months ago, I had to physically push through a wave of sheepishness and self-consciousness I hadn't felt—especially with her—in years. It took me a moment, but I succeeded.

I led her to my device.

"It's really pretty simple in concept." I surprised myself with how steady my voice was, how gentle. "You face it like this." I stood her toward the arced "back" of it. "See how your legs fit in these curves? Yes, you have to part them a little."

I might have even succeeded in being ominous, because Anna's face darkened around her smile as she moved, her expression narrowing from amusement to intrigue. I loved that subtle metamorphosis.

We each had our harbingers.

I pushed her gently forward, so that her upper thighs fit in the wooden channels. Anna had to move her feet just about shoulder width apart on the floor to fit right, her loose skirt easily letting her. That skirt came down to just above her knees, showing me stockinged calves. As she put her weight against the wood, it gave a low creaking sound and rocked a bit.

"That sounds...sturdy," she said, sarcastically.

I grinned. "I wanted it to make sounds." I reached to a side of the device and pulled a lever, resulting in a deep, wooden thunking sound. Anna's expression told me she felt it against her legs. The slight rocking of the shape stopped as it locked.

"Let me guess," she said, turning her head to give me a crooked smile as she leaned forward over the contoured top of the thing. My eyes followed her body as she settled. The curves I'd sculpted into the wood from memory of body and hands were as good as I could have hoped for. Anna's belly, chest, shoulders fit as if cradled, and her hands reached forward for the two polished grips.

She knew what she was doing, moving slowly, languidly, seductively for me. And the curve of the thing raised her ass just so...

"What was that, darling?" she asked, a wicked smile in her voice.

I had groaned without realizing it.

"Oh, that is so beautiful," I replied, gloating and glowing at the near realization of my concept. I'd have to show her the sketches later, but she put my drawings to shame. "Hold it right there. Just a couple more things."

I pushed on a polished panel beside the handholds and pulled out the short coil of leather I'd stored there, unfurling a cuff that I attached to her wrist as she watched. I could see the slight shudder that went though her body as I closed the cuff because I was looking for it. Her other hand loosened on the grip, as if she was going to pull it away, before I gently caught it and placed it in another cuff from the other side. Anna's breathing quickened, as had mine. We'd played games like this before, though not quite like this.

"What are you up to, Laz?" I heard that tiny quaver in her voice. That first hint of the Anna only I know, coming to visit. My lack of answer was another hint of the Lazslo only she knows.

I moved behind her and pulled two more broad leather straps from their hiding places, fitting them simultaneously around the hollows at the back of each of her knees. I let my fingers linger on the sheer fabric covering her legs, feeling her flex them and test the bonds a second after it was too late. I knew she was pulling at the cuffs, as well. I'd made them so that there was just a little bit of play, enough to give, I'd hoped, the smallest illusion—or temptation—of freedom of motion.

"I've had enough of midlife crises, Anna. I've decided to concentrate on the now, not looking forward or back. I asked myself, what do I want right now?"

I tried to sound detached, analytic. I failed.

"And you came up with a giant violin scroll?"

I looked at her on my construction, frowning in concentration.

"Mmm. It was really the curled arm of an antique chair that inspired me, but yes, the violin works, as well."

"And this is what you want?"

"It's part of it."

"And are there other parts, then?"

I ran my hand up her thigh, bunching her skirt until I found the top band of her thigh-highs. My eyes followed higher to her skirted hips and upraised rear.

"Ohh, yes. Yes."

My fingers itched. Not yet. Anna let out a sound—a cross between a sigh and a whimper—that made me salivate.

One more strap, a thin leather belt that went around her waist above her hips. Just strong and snug enough to hold her against the wood.

"Oh, Lazslo." How I loved the way her voice changed. "It's holding me like a big hand. It feels...made for me."

"It is." I released the lever I'd first pulled, making another satisfying *thunk*. The curl of wood groaned and rocked forward, pulling Anna off her feet. She gasped as her footing vanished, her hands jerking for support on the handgrips, before settling into the odd rolling sensation as the device found a new balance point.

I spent a moment letting the reality of it all sink in. Anna— my own Anna now—perfectly situated on my own device. Part of it, even. The one part that had been missing. A deep breath, as Anna watched me watching her. Her sometimes-haughty expression was now much more guarded as she waited for what I was going to do next.

"You have too many clothes on, Anna," I said. We had both used that line on each other more than once over the years. Usually it resulted in a laugh, followed by hands—one or two pairs—moving to remedy the situation. This time Anna's response was a quiet moan and a tug on the leather restraints. My device creaked under her.

Both Anna and I have learned a certain amount of foresight. Anna's skirt, sensible and conservative, was buttoned at the side, and she'd taken the care to leave it one button past nominal modesty. It was an easy thing to undo the rest of them, unwrap her and slide the opened fabric from under her, revealing lace-edged thigh-highs and plain, if pretty, panties. As I removed her shoes—there's only so much kicking one can do if bound at the knee—the rounded base of the device creaked and rocked with Anna's movements. Anna tensed under my fingers as she rocked back farther than she expected.

"Jesus, Lazslo, this thing isn't going to flip backward and crush me to death, is it?" The edge to Anna's voice was almost pissed off. Either she truly lacked confidence in my carpentry skills, or the disequilibrium was having a real effect.

"I don't think so, Anna," I replied, unreassuringly. In truth, I had no doubts at all, but I enjoyed Anna off balance. I chuckled at the thought, because I knew the sentiment was mutual. We've played with each other a long time, after all.

I took hold of the side of the wooden arm that extended under the handgrips and heaved up, as if really trying to flip the device. Anna's face betrayed a momentary shock as she cursed and grabbed the grips. Her heels barely touched the floor before I let up my effort, and she rocked back and forth for a while.

"No, I don't think so."

"Laz—" She did sound pissed now. I *had* scared her, just a little.

"Don't worry, Anna, I promise you're safe—from this, anyway."

Anna just looked at me, starting to go quiet, shadowed. Beautiful.

There are limits to foresight; Anna's shirt, bra and panties all presented removal problems. I could have slipped her top off by releasing one arm at a time. She might even have acquiesced, though likely not after my rocking tease. Besides, this wasn't about asking cooperation. Not after that last strap was secure. Fortunately, my workshop held a fair number of useful tools, and Anna had changes of clothes in her overnight bag.

I pulled my ridiculously large-for-the-task leather cutting shears off the wall. The first slide of the blade bottom against the skin of her back resulted in a sharp intake of breath, with a "Lazslo!" as the shears took their first bite of shirt and bra strap together. I methodically, silently, cut her top into enough ribbons to slide out from between her skin and the polished wood; she said nothing else as I did it. There really is something about destroying clothing. For a moment I paused, entertaining the idea of getting her bag and cutting up everything else she'd brought, right in front of her. I imagined Anna was thinking along the same lines when her body shivered under the half-closed blade.

With the shreds of her top littering my floor, I turned to her panties. One snip by each thigh and an easy pull. Smooth cotton, new; wet in the crotch. I decided to leave the stockings. They were, we both knew, one of my many personal weaknesses.

"That's much better." I said, watching Anna breathe, not quite panting yet. I walked around to where she could turn her head to see me as I undressed. I didn't make a show of it, but I did watch her eyes follow the revelation of my skin. My cock, hard since she first stretched out on my device, sprang free from my boxers in an almost comical manner, but neither of us was laughing now. "Much better," I repeated. Anna's eyes flashed dark as she licked her lips. A small bead of perspiration graced her temple.

I stepped over to the utility sink and filled a clean glass with water, taking a sip myself before coming over to offer it to her.

She shook her head, declining. I shrugged and set the glass on one of the worktables, then came back to beautiful Anna bent over the thing I'd made for her. I grasped the main lever once again and rocked her gently back and forth.

"The rocker can go both ways," I said, using my best pedantic voice. "I can let you back down onto your feet, or I can go the other way." Dark wood creaked as I demonstrated.

"How...convenient." Anna's hands gripped hard as I moved her. Her quip lost its sarcastic bite in the huskiness of her voice.

"Oh, it's not mere convenience, Anna. It's art. I mean, look at you. You're stunning." I paused to take in her whole length appreciatively before bending to whisper in her ear. "Did you know I made the straps just strong enough to hold you? There's even the chance I miscalculated and you could break free if you really tried."

I stepped back and continued. "Art and design, form and function. Really just this one lever can move the entire thing with a little effort, raising you right up to my mouth, so I can give you a good kiss without having to bend over."

I pushed the lever, holding its stop, ratcheting the big internal wooden gears loudly as Anna's rear end raised higher and higher. Her hands almost reached the floor as the wooden curve rolled under her. Each bump of the gears was designed to jar the solid structure, and I felt it do so through my free hand, just below Anna's side.

"Jesus, Laz. You're just e-evil." I believed from her voice that she felt and heard everything as I'd intended it. It thrilled me, and made my cock twitch in anticipation.

"Now I can give you all the preparation you need easily," I said, stepping back behind her. God, it was perfect. Anna's ass was right up in the air, her parted legs revealing her pink, swollen cunt at exactly my mouth level. I leaned in just a little bit to inhale her spicy sweetness, and was unable to stop until my lips pressed against her and my tongue was diving. We groaned together as I feasted like a man who hadn't eaten proper food in months. In a way, I hadn't. It took minutes before I could pull myself away, minutes in which Anna's cunt flooded against my tongue, and her muscles twitched and clutched at me when I stuck it as deep in her as I could. Her gasps and coos were hypnotic enough that I could have continued hours just listening to them. But I had other plans.

"Not"—I was close to panting now, too, pulling my head from between her thighs—"that you really needed any extra lubrication there, dear Anna, but this way I can get your ass ready, too." A single squeeze of the release handle and the whole device clunked back one loud step, presenting Anna's tight little pucker to me. Anna made a squeaking sound at the sudden jerk, and then another as I reverently placed each of my hands on her soft cheeks and pulled them apart, to allow my tongue to delve and dig once again against this more resistant opening. Anna's sounds were different, too, more distressed at first, then more base and guttural. I felt the rumbling of two awakening beasts now, hers as well as mine.

I loved the way she squirmed each time I forced my tongue into her, but my saliva wasn't going to be enough, if it came down to it. I pulled away and opened another little panel set flush in the smooth-faced wood between her legs. Hidden within was a container of lubricant—practical, if mundane. All Anna could know of what I was doing was what the vibrations and clicking of the opening and closing of the panel told her, until I spread her cheeks again and added a cool, generous dollop of the stuff right where it needed to be.

"Lazslo... What—what do you have planned?"

I could hear her trying to collect herself, instinctively trying to reassert control over herself and the situation. We were both given to that, and both of us, sometimes, needed to be broken of it.

"I'm not sure yet, Anna," I lied, and she knew it.

I wiggled my index finger past her clenching sphincter, pushing the lube up her clutching back passage as a moan pushed from her lips.

"We're going to play a game. The game of 'Which Hole?'"

"Wh—?" Before she could fully respond, I released the lever, and let the groaning, clacking device roll her back down. Whatever the question on her lips had been died as she lowered back into place, and turned into a sharp inhalation as her descending cunt met my upturned cockhead.

"Which hole, Anna?" I asked, taking hold of the main lever and rocking her back just a little farther, the head of my cock slipping up from her split labia to kiss up against her anus.

"Which hole should I fuck? Which should I come in?" I pushed the lever, sliding my cock back to nudge her cunt open just the tiniest bit.

"You're not… "

"No, not today, my pet. This game is high stakes."

"Oh, Lazslo…" Reproach colored her voice, castigating me for the breach. We always used protection; except for those times Anna had been on the pill for herself or other lovers, it was a hard and fast rule. Except for that one time we swore we'd never repeat, it was a given we'd both lived with since our first time together, and I'd just broken it. And it wasn't just that. I'd tongued her rear end before, fingered her, even slid two up her backside while I went down on her, all to wonderful effect. But in all our time together, I'd only fucked her ass once, when we were both stoned nearly mad, and that had been less than satisfying for both of us. We'd always had enough other limits to push, other boundaries of pleasure to explore, that this one always slid by.

Anna's muscles flexed—legs, arms. She tested the strength of her bonds in earnest, and I listened to the leather and wood creak as she strained. I rocked her gently back and forth, my cock nudging her ass, then her cunt, and back again. Her sounds changed as I pressed against each entrance.

"This—ah! This isn't fair, Lazslo." I heard how upset, even angry, she was. But underneath it...underneath it was that tremble, and each time my cock slid between her cunt lips, it sluiced into a new flood of her juices. I knew if I looked there'd be a veritable rivulet dripping down the wood between her legs.

"No. It's not." I said. Butterflies turned in my own stomach—something I hadn't felt in a long time. Transgression. We both knew I was, right now, changing something that had been a comfortably edgy, stably twisted given for each of us for over twenty years. I'd thought about this for a long time.

"Tell me, Anna, which one are you more fearful of?"

"I'm not afraid of you, Lazslo," she whispered.

"Liar." God, I wanted it to be a lie. And I wanted it to be the truth at the same time. The turbulence of that conflict and the others within me—within her—was the Now I sought, a place and time where everything outside the sphere of the physical senses and base reactions was just static. "Pick."

Maybe she *was* afraid. Or just mad, or defiant. Whatever the case, she didn't answer as I rocked her back and forth, the wood creaking deeply, ominously, but her body told me what I wanted to know. It was the way she tensed whenever my cock slid up and settled in to press against that lubed hole, and the little whimper she couldn't suppress.

"I think it's...yes," I locked the lever in place, feeling the sharp snap of the wooden ratchet even through Anna's body. She groaned and shook her head as my cock stopped sliding and instead nuzzled against the little pucker of her ass. Until that moment, I hadn't decided what *I* had wanted more: to fuck Anna bareback, and play the serious game of roulette, or to take her ass—really take her—for the first time. However, when I heard that first soft, high-pitched keen as I tested her, it all collapsed into a single driving want. I positively hummed.

"Anna. Have you any idea what a *gratifying* sound that is to hear from you? How I love hearing it?" I think she knew, because she shuddered and pulled hard again at the leather. I brought my hands back to each of her cheeks, digging in just a little and pulling them apart. *Fuck*, the sight of that "forbidden" connection, the menacing potential of it, the feel of being poised right there—it made me boil. I leaned gently forward.

"I'm not going to fuck you—yet. I'm going to let gravity do the work first." I kept speaking, because we both like words. "God, Anna, I got the angle just perfect. The only thing keeping me out right now is the resistance of your muscles."

Anna groaned, her whole body clenched.

"It's true. With all that slippery stuff, I should slide right in to you. I *feel* you all tense and closed under my hands, against my cock. But you're already shaking with the effort of keeping me out."

Everything about this scene said I was doing something wrong, something bad. I didn't care. Hell, the exultation, even gloating, in my voice was pretty clear. Anna, I'm sure, heard it, too.

"D-damn you, Lazslo." Her teeth clenched as she spoke.

"I know, love. I know," I said soothingly, disingenuously. "You have me so damn wound up. I want to fuck you so bad, so *hard*. I'm aching for it, Anna. But I won't—I can't start until you've let me in. All the way in."

By now I was almost not recognizing my own voice from the tension in it, and I knew it was affecting her, as well. This game of word and want is what we played, though I'd raised the stakes unilaterally this time. "Anna, it's no small act of will, on my part, not to grab your hips and just force myself into you."

I let my hands slide up to caress and settle gently into the familiar, delicious swell of her hips. Her moan choked into a gasp followed by held breath. It *would* be so easy. But no. I dragged my fingers back to her ass and spread it again. Had the head of my cock made just a little progress, her passage giving and opening just a little for me?

"We have all the time in the world, Anna. Whenever you're ready, just let me in. Just a little bit. If you relax your ass, I'll start to sink in, and it will all take care of itself."

"It's g-going to hurt."

"It might, Anna. Less if you let go."

"God!"

"God is right. You look so fucking heavenly from here. Your whole backside is a temple, my Anna."

"F-fucking cliché."

I chuckled. I couldn't help it. And Anna's ass trembled and relaxed the smallest bit.

"N—!"

"Ohhh, yes, Anna. I'm in the perfect place. Fight it as much as you want."

She did—oh, how she did. Every millimeter was a struggle of renewed frantic efforts, clenching her ass, pulling at her bonds. I was so sensitized and attentive to that junction that I felt everything. My breathing changed, deepening as I felt and watched my flared head pushing her inexorably open. Every new nerve touched as I penetrated her seemed to result in a new, tremulous whimper from her.

"You know it's inevitable, Anna. We both do."

She shook her head, but the groan that came from her wasn't of denial. Another followed it, lower pitched, as the widest part of my cockhead made its way past her failing resistance.

"Oh, Anna, this is so wrong. So hot. I mean how can you let this rigid thing into your ass? Look at your muscles distending around my shaft. It's just awful. But there it is; I'm almost there. You're flaring open around me." My voice was rough enough almost to be a growl.

"Lazslo—" It was almost a whine, followed by a little grunt as my cockhead passed into her and her ring muscle closed around it.

"Mm, that's it, Anna. That's it."

"It...it hurts, Laz."

"Relax."

"I..."

"Try. Relax and it'll go easier." We were both educated. We knew the truth and limitations of that statement, and what her relaxing would mean.

I felt her. Her muscles fluttered, squeezing, trying to prevent entry, pushing to expel me, and, when she could assert the control, relaxing to let me slip deeper. It was an exquisite battle to feel around my cock, to see in the shaking and sweat of her body, to hear in the ragged breath and tortured sounds coming from her throat. I slid my hands up to rest on Anna's rump as gravity brought me into her.

As I bored in, the contractions of her muscles mattered less and less, though they still affected how quickly I impaled her. Anna's sounds changed, too, coming deeper from her chest as my cock found its way deeper into her ass. When my legs first touched hers, they were trembling even though they weren't supporting her weight.

"Oh, Anna, can you feel me? My cock loves this so much."

"Yess…you're taut as a spring."

"I'm trying not to fuck you like an animal. Just yet. Not until I'm all the way in."

"And then…"

"And then I'm going to let it all go, Anna. Everything. I promise." This time it was my teeth that were gritted.

"Oh, yes, Lazslo." Fuck. There it was. That tone in her voice. Beyond hunger or fear.

Then, for the last few moments there was silence, except for our labored breathing. I slid my hands up Anna's back, sweat-slick now as my hips first touched and then pressed into the flesh of her ass. My eyes were half-closed, and I imagined hers were, too. When I felt my weight settle against her, my cock buried in the squeezing heat of her ass, I groaned louder than the creak of the wood, and she hummed, laying her head on the smooth wood between her outstretched, slack arms.

My hands reached her shoulders and gave her a masseur's squeeze before dragging gently back down over her sides to settle on her hips once more. This time, as my fingers found their grip there, it was with purpose and finality. Anna knew that grip well. I closed my eyes, just feeling everything. Potential. Inevitability. The forever and ephemeral nature of this moment—of us two here, now.

"Anna," I whispered.

"Yes, Lazslo," she responded, equally quiet.

"I'm going to fuck you now. Fuck your ass. Until…" My words trailed off because my heart was hammering too fast to figure out what to say. I heard a sound. It might have been her; it might have been me.

I heard another sound. It might have been "Show me." It might have.

THE NECKCLOTH

Annabel Joseph

The Countess of Waverly backed across the candlelit bedroom. "If you were a gentleman, you would not do this."

Her husband chuckled. "If you were a lady, there would be no need."

He strode toward her, a column of stark black and pristine white formal evening clothes. She scrambled behind a settee, gathering up her pink silk skirts with her heart beating in her throat. "I did not write that letter to Lord Eversham. I swear to you, I didn't write it."

"My dear, your perfume was all over it." He flicked the paper in his hand. "As was your atrocious handwriting. You are caught." He surveyed the chintz-upholstered settee between them. "Do not infuriate me by making me chase you."

She feinted left, but he moved right and caught her easily. Curse him, he knew all her tricks. His hands fastened on her shoulders and he gave her a little shake. "Eversham, Posey? *Eversham?* If you must throw yourself at one of my contemporaries, let it be someone worthy of your"—he threw a look down her plunging bodice—"prodigiously wanton charms."

She cracked him across the cheek.

"Oh, do it again with the glove off," he murmured. "That was pathetic."

She ripped off both gloves in a temper and pushed against his chest. "You are so cruel to me, Thomas. You mock me. You ignore me and run around London with your friends. At least Eversham notices me. You only notice me when I'm bad."

"Someone has to keep you in line, wife. Now, you will kindly untie my neckcloth."

"No," she cried. "I will not."

His fingers tightened on her arms. "If I have to send for my valet to do it, I will allow him to stay and watch what happens next."

"Oh, I hate you." But she knew he was a man of his word, so she did as he asked. Her fingers trembled, moving through the copious folds of starched white linen to locate the knot.

"The pin first," he reminded her.

"I know."

"We have been through this enough times." He tilted his chin so she could slide her fingers inside his collar. "You should be an expert at neckcloth removal by now."

She hissed as the end of the pin pricked her finger.

"Let me see," he said.

She held up the injured digit. He kissed it and slipped the pearl-tipped pin into a pocket. "You'll live. Proceed."

She blinked and pouted and went back to her task. From time to time, her knuckles brushed against the fair stubble on his cheeks. He was tall and blond, haughty and handsome. Posey knew that other ladies talked about her husband behind their fans. They whispered that he was sinfully pleasant to look at, a fine figure of a man.

They didn't know what he was like behind closed doors.

"The longer you take, the more time I have to hone my jealous outrage." He shook his head as she unraveled the intricate folds. "*Eversham*. I cannot countenance it. I really cannot."

"Eversham has kind eyes," she said with a sniff. "So much kinder than yours."

His pale blue gaze fell on her like ice chips. She swallowed hard and focused on her task. When she nearly had it loose he drew her fingers away and unwound the remainder of the neckcloth himself.

"Undress," he said, his fingers sliding down his coat to pop open the buttons. His waistcoat followed, thrown over a chair. He scowled when she didn't jump to obey him. "Undress or I shall do it for you, and you seem to dislike that."

"Because you always rip my dress!"

"I bought it," he said, turning his attention to his shirt buttons. "I buy all your clothing. I will rip it however and whenever I wish."

Oh, he was intolerable. But this gown was her favorite so she decided to obey. She put her fingers to the fastenings she could reach and grudgingly accepted his help with the rest. He stared in a lurid and ungentlemanly fashion as she shimmied out of the dress.

"Everything. Underthings. Stockings," he said when she paused. "Have I ever let you keep anything on?"

She stripped down to absolutely nothing, muttering to herself about the trials of being married to an uncivilized tyrant.

"Give me your hands," he said. "Hold them out before you."

She did, with the greatest reluctance. Was it so bad to write a letter? A tame one at that?

"I am going to run away to my father." She glared at him as

he wound the neckcloth about her wrists. "I will tell him exactly how you treat me."

"You did that," he reminded her, tying the cloth and leaving the tails free. "He sent you right back. And what happened then?" He poked a finger in the air. "Ah, I remember. I tied you to the bedpost with my neckcloth and whipped your bottom with a birch rod."

He put a hand at the small of her back and led her forward toward the same mahogany bedpost. She hated this post with a vengeance. By now her nails had scratched multiple marks into the ornately carved wood. *If you were not such a naughty wife...*

She stared straight ahead as he fixed the loose ends of the neckcloth around the post with a smartly tied square knot. "I hate you," she whispered with venom. "That is why I write to other men."

"You write to other men because you lack discipline, my dear. But do not fear. Discipline is my specialty." He reached beneath the bed for the bundled birch rod. "I had the groundskeeper freshen this with new twigs. Perhaps you will feel the difference."

"This is not fair," she cried. "If only you loved me! You would not treat me this way."

"To the contrary," he said, the warmth of his chest brushing her back. "I treat you this way because I *do* love you. Eversham shall not have you. No other man shall. You are mine."

She felt a shuddery pleasure uncoil at his closeness, at the threat of him towering over her from behind. He brushed aside her coiffed red curls to press a kiss at her nape, his other hand sliding down the curve of her spine.

"I never had it in mind to marry someone so wayward, my naughty young wife." She jumped as his palm opened against her backside and delivered a sharp slap. "But I'll be damned if I'll let you walk all over me."

She tensed as he squeezed her buttocks and smacked both cheeks again in quick succession. "I don't mean to be bad. I'm sorry."

"You are always sorry when it gets to this point."

She tugged at the neckcloth as he lifted the birch rod. She hated the pain of his birchings. The whip and sting and—

"Do not pull at that neckcloth, dearest. If you tear it, there will be hell to pay."

She shrank forward against the bedpost, her whipping post, burying her face against the linen that held her trapped. The neckcloth smelled of his scents of spice and cologne. "Please," she cried. "I will not be naughty again."

"I sincerely hope not." *Thwack!*

She shrieked and went up on her toes. "No. No, please!"

"Oh yes, my dear." *Thwack!* The birch rod caught her across both cheeks, a burning, smarting stroke of fire. *Thwack!*

"I cannot—oh—I cannot bear it, husband. Please!"

"The time to think about whether or not you could bear it"— *Thwack!*—"was before you wrote that letter to Lord Eversham. You knew what the penalty would be if you were caught."

"I did not intend to get caught!"

He chuckled and tapped the backs of her thighs. "Stop shrinking away from your justly earned punishment. Position yourself properly. Present your bottom to me as you've been taught."

She gripped her linen bonds in desperation. "I cannot. Do you think I'm made of iron?"

"I think you're made of sugar, sweeting. Bottom out now, or you shall receive double the strokes."

She stamped her feet, not that it would be of any use. At least he would know what an unfair ogre he was. She hung on the neckcloth, sticking her bottom out as much as she dared in her situation. *Thwack!*

It was too much to withstand. She spun about and danced sideways. "No, please, no. If you will persist in these cruelties—"

"I will persist," he said, raising his voice. "I will persist until you have been adequately punished for your transgression." He flung the birch on the bed and considered her with his arms crossed over his chest. "This will not do at all." He scanned the room until his eyes lit on her stockings. She watched with a sense of dread as he went to pick them up.

"What are you doing? Those are my favorite stockings."

"That is my favorite neckcloth. We shall endeavor not to destroy one another's favorite things." The stockings came around her waist. Wrapped together, they made a formidable restraint. He knotted them hard at the small of her back. "That will keep the middle still," he said. She felt his fingers in her hair then, pulling and twisting. He tilted her head back for a kiss. "You will not be needing this." The pile of her curls fell down as he drew a ribbon from the auburn mass.

He knelt and trapped her ankles, even though she kicked at him. He was stronger than her. It was no great thing for him to cinch them to the bottom of the post with the wide velvet ribbon. He stood back and surveyed his work. "Much better."

Posey squirmed helplessly in her bonds. The neckcloth held her hands fast. The wool stockings scratched at her waist, while the ribbon formed a binding vise about her ankles. She could not move an inch in any direction.

She could not get away.

"Now," her husband said, "I can punish you as you deserve."

"Oh, please," she begged, but there was no mercy in his gaze.

"Eyes forward. I needn't tell you to assume the position. You're not going anywhere."

Thwack! Somehow the pain was heightened by the fact that she couldn't escape it. Each swish of the birch rod found its mark—the throbbing, heated pillow of her hindquarters. By the second stroke she began to sob. By the fifth, she was soaking his favorite linen neckcloth with tears. "Please, please stop," she begged. "I will never write another gentleman. I will never so much as look at Eversham again."

"I should hope not." *Thwack!*

"Please! How can I prove that I have reformed?" *Thwack!*

"Ow! Please, I will do anything to show my remorse. To show I have…"

He lowered the birch.

"To show I have lear—learned my lesson," she stammered through tears. "I'll do anything." Her voice faded to a whisper as she slumped against the post.

"Anything, wife?"

"Anything. Even…even that thing I don't like to do."

He made a soft sound. "Even that? You are remorseful indeed." He was still a moment, then he sighed, knelt and slid the birch rod under the bed. "Very well. In that case, I suppose it's fortunate you are so well restrained."

She heard him cross to the bureau and slide open a drawer. The rattle of a glass jar was followed by the drawer easing shut again. He undid the falls of his trousers, took them down and laid them aside. His member was stiff and reddish-purple, jutting out in front of him. Posey whimpered and closed her eyes. "Please, do not be slow and meticulous about it. Do not make me wait."

He returned to her, stood behind her and caressed her smarting bottom, poking his hard length against her back. "This is not a thing I can do quickly. You know that by now."

She arched her hips forward, so the wicked, tingling pearl at her center contacted the mahogany post. "Please don't hurt me, Thomas."

"Then relax for me." Deft fingers slid down the crevice of her bottom to the tight, secret place he sought. He reached for the jar and pressed a dollop of the slick cream at the opening. She pushed back against his fingers, moaning at the dull ache of penetration. The stockings scratched her as she wiggled her hips.

"Be still," he whispered, "or I will bring out the birch rod again."

She tightened her fingers in the starched white neckcloth and squeezed her eyes shut as he palmed her buttocks and parted them wide. He pressed the head of his phallus against her tight hole, gently at first, then more insistently.

She couldn't move an inch to evade him.

"Oh...Thomas..." He slid in a bit farther. There was building, terrifying discomfort, but no real pain. He reached around to cup her breasts, the roughness of his cheeks scratching across her temple and jaw.

"If you were not such a bad girl, we would not have to do this," he said.

"I know," she replied mournfully.

He slid deeper. She felt the tight orifice give way and admit her husband's thick rod. He eased slowly into her trapped, helpless body, inside that shameful place. She was pinned from behind now, restrained by her husband in the deepest possible way.

"You are not grinding on the bedpost, are you, dearest?" he asked. "We talked about how inappropriate that is."

"I am not," she gasped, pressing her hips forward. "It's only that when you thrust deep inside me, it pushes me against the post right...right there."

"Ah. So it cannot be helped."

"No. No, sir, it cannot."

She drew in a deep shuddering breath, closing her teeth on the cloth that smelled of her husband. Her ankles fought the grip of the ribbon as she arched on her toes. "Please, sir," she said between pants. "If you really want to punish me, you should not be so gentle and slow. You should feel free to give me the harsh treatment I deserve."

His fingers tightened on her nipples in a worsening pinch. "It was a terrible thing to write that letter to Eversham," he said, his pace quickening. He drove in and out of her bottom in rough, short strokes. Her naughty button was forced against the bedpost in a most arousing rhythm.

"You are really teaching me a lesson now," she sighed. "I am so very sorry. So very sorry. So very—" She gritted her teeth and threw her head back as he thrust to the hilt inside her. She felt the neckcloth give way as an orgasm built and broke wide within her, sharp pulsations of pleasure originating in her bottom and turning her entire body inside out. Her husband bucked and groaned behind her, driving deep in the throes of his own release.

He put his hands over hers. They both breathed deeply and spasmodically for long moments.

"God, Tom," she said, going limp against the post. "Holy hell."

He sighed as he licked a trail across her shoulder. "That was the best one yet."

"I agree," she said. "Even better than the medieval wedding night."

"By far."

He withdrew from her, his hands circling her waist, running over the authentic reproduction Victorian-era wool stockings they'd purchased online. "These feel kinda scratchy."

"They are. But the birch rod feels worse."

"Good thing you're a maso," he said, a smile playing at the corner of his lips.

"It is a good thing. You were whaling on me at the end there." She wiggled her wrists in the neckcloth. "I think I ripped this. Actually, I'm sure I did."

"Bad girl. You'll have to be punished. Or..." He slapped her ass. "We can buy another one on eBay."

"At this rate, I'll have to learn how to make them myself. This is the third one this month."

"Either that, or we move on to another era." They looked at each other, then back at the neckcloth drooping from the post.

"Not yet," she said. "I'll learn how to make them. It can't be that hard."

"You do that. I'll assemble a few more birch rods." He grinned at her, slipping a hand down to cup her slick pussy. "Eversham shall not have you!"

"Not ever?"

"Not ever." He kissed the curve of her neck. "You're mine, my naughty, naughty wife."

ANYWAY

Sommer Marsden

I was stuck.

I wiggled my arms and tried not to panic. It wasn't a big deal. Not really. Mason was just in the next room brushing his teeth. But still, I'd have to admit I was stuck. Take the teasing…

I struggled some more.

I was just starting to sweat when I heard that dark chuckle, felt my skin rise up in a revolt of gooseflesh at his warm velvet voice. "Having some trouble there, Robin?"

I glanced up, gave him a fake laugh. "No. It's fine. I'm just…" He watched as I pushed my arms against the wall. How could I be this solidly stuck in the arms of a jacket? Even worse, how could I be in the position to have to admit it and ask for help?

He stood there smirking. His amusement became too much for me and tears pricked my eyes. "Goddamn it! Your mother's like a fucking bird. Why did I even think to try this on?"

I wiggled my shoulders and felt the fabric give just a tiny bit, sliding down my forearms. But it wasn't much. They were trapped behind me pretty tightly, caught in too snug, thick fabric that didn't want to yield. My arms remained bound behind my back, cinched by unforgiving velvet jacket arms.

"Do you need help?"

"Yes! No!" I moved some more, feeling the bite of stiffness in my shoulders from having my arms so far back. "This is fucking ridiculous!"

Panic had set in. All I could think about was what if he hadn't been home? What if I'd been alone? What the fuck then?

Mason stepped close to me, crowding my personal space. I froze. He smiled down at me. His brown eyes were amused; his thin but kissable lips followed the sentiment. "Would you like me to help you?"

I was nude but for a pair of lavender lace panties and some argyle kneesocks, of all things. We were supposed to just go out and grab a cheesesteak or pizza for dinner. I was supposed to be throwing on some clothes. Instead I'd dove into the bag of castoffs his mother had given me. She was a foot shorter and twenty-five pounds lighter than me. Why she insisted on giving me her clothing rejects was beyond me. Why I always insisted on torturing myself by trying them on was even more baffling.

He was waiting. Watching me. I continued to wriggle like a fish on a hook even as he calmly observed.

He put his hand on my belly. Spread his fingers wide. I stilled. "Robin. Would you like me to help you?" he asked once more.

I sucked in a breath, feeling his fingers on my skin and the stiffening of my nipples, which he noted with a quick glance and a small smile.

"I..." Why wasn't I saying yes? "She's so freakishly skinny," I said by way of answer.

He nodded. "My mother is petite."

"Why does she give me her clothes?" I watched him watching

me, and my heart thumped in my chest. A caged thing that wanted to be set free.

"I have no idea." He reached up and pinched my nipple between his fingertips. Fiery lust blazed through me.

I wanted to touch him. To be touched. So I said, "Yes, please help me out."

His eyebrow went up, and a smirk played across his lips. He bent, eyes still on mine, and sucked my other nipple into the damp heat of his mouth. He sucked hard, and I felt the echo of that pleasurable draw on my flesh as far down as my cunt.

Mason had forgotten dinner. I could tell by the look in his eyes. I'd seen that look before, when he wielded a paddle, or just his bare hand, or even a crop. My stomach dropped like I was falling, my breath quick in my throat.

"Please," I said. But even I wasn't so convinced.

He drew a finger down the middle of me from chest to mound, then stopped to cup my pussy through my panties. His smile had turned dangerous. "I don't know."

I struggled, panic flaring hotly inside me. Small beads of sweat dotted my upper lip, and I licked them away.

"Mason—"

He leaned in and kissed me. His tongue slid along mine, tangling, bullying. I sighed against his mouth and felt him smile.

"I was going to tie you up later, anyway. I think you've done a fairly decent job of immobilizing yourself for me."

I gasped—both from the fact that his fingers had slipped between my nether lips, and that they'd driven the lace of my knickers against my swollen clitoris. "You're not going to leave me like this, are you?"

There was begging in my voice. We could both hear it. It amused him; I knew because he laughed softly and shook his head.

"Why *did* you try it on?" he asked, straightening up. He moved behind me, and his fingers skated along my bunched-up shoulder muscles. His touch was both infuriating and insanely pleasurable.

"I have no idea. I'm a moron?"

"You do it every time. Try stuff on, get angry, rant, donate it."

"Again, I ask, why does she give it to me?" I countered.

He poked his head over my shoulder and said in my ear, "Because like her son, she sometimes gets off on inflicting pain."

That shut me up. It was torture to try on my mother-in-law's hand-me-downs. They were always so nice, so fashionable and too fucking small and yet...I kept doing it.

"Mean," I humphed.

"Controlling," he laughed.

I felt him test the restrictive white cloth that still had me stuck good and tight. Another rush of anxiety worked through me and I tried to breathe. Tried not to beg. But finally I gave in. "Jesus, Mason, please."

"Like I said," he went on as if I hadn't spoken. "I was going to tie you up anyway." His hand skimmed over the swell of my ass. He plucked at the lavender lace that covered my bottom.

"But...I..."

"And here you were such a good girl and did it for me." His teeth captured my earlobe and he nipped me. Wetness graced the inside of my panties, want flexed deep in my pussy. I sighed.

"But..."

"So what I think I'll do instead is...this." He moved to stand in front of me, pushed me down slowly but insistently by my now-singing shoulders. The sockets ached, my muscles screamed for relief, and yet, when I went down on my knees, I grew wetter.

I opened my mouth without being asked, and he stuck his finger in. Then a second. I sucked them like I would his cock as he watched me, smiling. "Good girl."

Heat flooded my cheeks.

I couldn't drag my eyes away as he undid the button on his jeans. His zipper. When he pulled his cock free and stroked it, a tremor of anticipation rocked me.

"I—" I pressed my lips together, with no idea what I was going to say.

Mason dragged the smooth warmth of his cockhead along my lips. I kept them pressed tight together almost petulantly until he grunted. Then I gave in to my own urge to have him in my mouth, to taste his skin.

I sucked just the tip, driving my tongue against the slick indentation at the tip. I tasted the salt of his precome and the sweetness of his shaft. I drove my mouth down slowly, dragging a big breath of air into my lungs as I did it. My knees started to ache and my shoulders started to scream. And yet, it was perfect. Just what I needed. My pussy flexed eagerly to confirm the emotion.

Mason held my head and slipped in and out, wetting my lips with my own saliva as he fucked my mouth. "I think, despite being a good girl, that maybe someone needs a spanking to remind her not to fall into my mother's passive-aggressive trap."

I blinked, then sucked with all my might, feeling the ache in my tongue and jaw from the exertion. A small spasm sounded inside me, a precursor to the orgasms I imagined to be on the way.

He remained silent long enough to make me worry. His big hands muffled the world by covering my ears as he drove into my mouth, filled my throat, took me the way he needed to find pleasure.

Behind my back, I clasped my hands together restlessly, thinking maybe I should just struggle and thrash to get the dreaded jacket down and off my arms. And then…what?

"Oh don't run away, sweetheart," he said, reading my mind. He brushed my bangs off my forehead, and cooler air kissed my damp skin. "You know you want it."

He pulled free of my mouth with a small pop and grinned.

I shivered. Because he was right. As miserable as I was trapped in this stupid jacket, I wanted it. I wanted him to thrust back into my mouth. I wanted him to flip me over and touch me. I wanted to feel the sting and kiss of his hands on me. I did. I wanted it.

I shook my head and tried to capture his cock with my mouth. He pulled back, shaking his head and pushing his jeans all the way down. Mason picked them up, draped them over a chair, started on the buttons of his shirt.

"Admit it, Robin," he said. "Say it."

I cocked my head, and it slipped out before I could help myself. "It."

He didn't smile.

"Okay. You get your wish." He stopped with the buttons and moved toward me fast. I watched, curious, until he walked past me, dropped to his knees and grabbed my wrists. I felt him begin to tug the fabric and pull it down.

"Wait!" I yelled and we both went still.

I said nothing. All I could hear was the tick of the hallway clock floating into our room.

"I'm waiting, Robin."

"I…don't…" I said, sighing. "Don't free me. Not yet. Please."

Was I insane? My arms and shoulders and back ached. Here I was staring freedom in the face, and I said no?

"Okay. But why?" I heard that smile on his face. It made me insane. Angry. Enraged. Offended! And fuck me hard...so turned on.

"I...want..." I hung my head, adding fresh agony to the back of my neck. "I want it!" I said, and then clenched my jaw so tight with frustration I thought I might break a few teeth.

Mason said nothing. Simply stood and removed his shirt. He bent, put his hands around me and helped me stand. He walked me to the bed, tipped me onto my belly so that my hips were on the mattress but my legs touched the floor, and stood behind me. I could feel him there between my thighs, crowding me, his hand coming down to stroke my lower back, the swell of my ass, the backs of my thighs.

Fire erupted on my skin from his gentle touch. My shoulders started to tremble. A tear slid from my eye, and I bit my lip.

"Hips," he said.

I lifted them willingly and he tugged my panties down slowly. He worked them over the swell of my hips, then whisked them away.

"You need to stop trying them on," he said conversationally. "For your sanity."

The blow landed suddenly and before I felt it, I heard it. Red-hot pain followed the sound, heat followed the pain, pleasure tagged along.

"And for mine," Mason said.

I nodded crazily against the dark-blue bedspread. I chewed my lip, tried not to sob, but found myself fixating on the clenching pleasure between my thighs.

"Say you will," he commanded. But then he delivered another heavy-handed swat.

My body rocked, bowed, and I tilted my head back before crying out. "I will."

"Promise," he ordered and then crossed the initial blow with another expert smack.

"Promise," I wheezed because the air rushed out of me.

I couldn't help it. Didn't even think of it. I clenched my cunt tight and a small blip of bliss coursed through me. I could come if we kept this up.

"Stop that," he said.

I did as told, though it was hard.

He knocked my legs apart with his knee and then leaned back over me, spreading my nether lips with his fingers. I wished I were faceup. I wished I could see him. I stopped wishing when he drove a few fingers into me.

He flexed them against the tender desperate place in me that needed friction. I tried to spread myself more for him. He put a hand on my ass, pressed down, held me steady and fucked me with his fingers for a few seconds. I could hear how wet I was. It made me blush.

"You are tall and curvy and luscious," he said softly.

I smiled—until he smacked my left asscheek hard enough to make me shout.

"My mother is short and thin and, as you noted, birdlike." One, two, three fast swats on my upper thighs just below my ass.

My heartbeat throbbed in my bottom and my clit thumped in time.

I moaned when he dropped to his knees, kissed the skin he'd just spanked and buried his face against my ass, finding my clit through my spread legs with his warm tongue. He only did it for a second. Just long enough for me to want it bad. And to suffer the loss of the sensation.

When Mason stood, he yanked the jacket binding my arms, sliding the too tight sleeves all the way down and freeing me.

This time when I moaned it was with painful pleasure to feel blood flowing back into my arms. It hurt. It felt wonderful.

"Roll on your back, Robin."

I rolled, feeling drunk with all the sensations. Feeling buzzed with sensory overload.

He quickly tied the jacket arms in one big sloppy knot around my wrists. He put my arms up over my head. "Spread your legs." His cock stood out hard and flushed and I wanted to suck it again, touch it, have it in me.

I licked my lips and did as he told me.

"I think that you've learned your lesson."

I nodded. "I have. I have." I was repeating myself, frantic, mindless with want.

"But I think it will stick with you if I give you a little more incentive to retain this memory."

He knelt next to me on the bed to my left and studied my face. I was confused but ready. Would he kiss me? Pinch me? Go down on me? What would he—

"Count to five," he said, and gave me a hard but not too hard spank to my pussy.

The blow rocked me not so much because it was rough but because it shocked me.

"One." Breathy, shocked.

A second spank.

"Two." Moaning. Tortured. "Three, four," I cooed, the sensation of his impact rocking through me.

The final smack was a bit harder. It startled my clitoris, which forced pleasure through my womb. "Five," I breathed.

He moved fast, his face intent, telling me he was done with the game. He was ready to move on. Mason moved between my thighs, kissed me, crushed his big body down on mine until all the air rushed out of me and then he kissed me some more. I was light-headed with the kiss and the need for air.

He shoved his hand under my ass and tilted me. The tender skin of my ass pounded like an extra heart from the rough contact, but when he pressed into me, filling me with his cock, I came on the first stroke. One single rough thrust and I was clenching up around him, saying his name over and over.

"Good girl," he laughed. I felt him grin against my cheek, realized how fucking much I loved him. Too much for my body to hold. Too big for one soul to comprehend.

"I love you," I told him. "I love you, I love you. And I love when you fuck me."

"I love you, too, sweetheart. I love you when you're bad and when you're good and when you help me out."

"Help you out?" I was trying to focus but another white-hot orgasm was rushing toward me. By the way he bucked against me I knew Mason was close—so, so close.

"Yeah. Like getting yourself all tangled up, blushing...mostly naked and pluckable." He pinched my ass when he said pluckable. "Like a ripe lush fruit."

I came with a loud sob. He covered my mouth with his, swallowed it down. "It gives me an excuse to do something I was going to do anyway."

"Like what?" I whispered.

His dark eyes flashed and he thrust once more, emptying into me with a rough grunt. He pressed his forehead against mine, moving just a little so small flares of pleasure warmed my cunt. "Like fuck my beautiful wife."

My stomach growled. We both laughed. "I think I'm hungry," I said.

Mason untied me. "If you can find something to wear—that *fits*—I'll take you to that dinner I promised."

"So no jacket from your mother?" I teased.

"Now I thought you'd learned your lesson." He kissed my neck.

"Oh, I did. But you'll forgive me if I forget it once in a while." I wouldn't say what we both knew. The part about it being on purpose.

"Don't worry. I'll just have to remind you."

I was counting on it.

EEL

Annabeth Leong

"Where's Ethan?" I asked Alicia. My friend sat curled in a folding chair tucked behind the play party's person-size speakers. I never would have found her if I hadn't been so sure she'd be there somewhere.

Alicia sighed theatrically, but beneath her dramatics, her lip trembled with genuine hurt. She wore a lacy set of lingerie we'd bought together the weekend before, and nothing else but makeup. Tear-streaked makeup.

Oh boy. I sank to the floor beside her chair. She'd rolled herself into such a tiny ball that our heads were almost level now. "What happened?" The music forced me to raise my voice, but I kept my tone as gentle as I could.

"Ethan says he's tired of getting embarrassed by an eel." I restrained a sigh of my own. Alicia, double-jointed and flexible enough that she performed with an amateur circus on weekends, had gained a reputation in the years we'd both been in the scene. I'd never met the top who could tie her in a way that held. And she liked guys with egos, who didn't take kindly to the way her antics challenged their status as scary, black-leather-wearing doms.

I reached up to pat her thigh, amazed as always at how slim it was. It wasn't actually smaller than my wrist, but I could easily have made the joke. Whenever I went out with Alicia, people would come up to me and ask if I was "the man," probably because I literally loom over her. I do prefer girls, but I don't normally feel quite that butch. Besides, Alicia could probably kick my ass if she wanted to. I may be big and strong, but she's a third-degree black belt in American jiujitsu and I've only made it to brown.

Add in her gorgeous black hair, Mediterranean skin and those big, black "Help me" eyes—so incongruous if you actually know Alicia—and my pretty little friend could ride roughshod over just about anybody's ego.

"Kristi, all I wanted was to come to this party and get tied up," Alicia wailed.

I cocked my head at her. In the past, I'd given her my best supportive answers, but at this point it seemed Alicia needed a dose of reality. "If you love being tied up so much, how come you never stay tied up?"

She pouted. "Now you sound like him."

"I want you to tell me the truth. Are you trying to embarrass your tops?"

She didn't answer with words, but a tiny smile started at the corners of her mouth. She must have seen my face change in response, because her eyes went wide and innocent.

"Let's give you the benefit of the doubt for a minute," I said, though privately I had my reservations. "What would you say you're looking for when you do your eel thing?"

Her forehead wrinkled and she propped her arms up on her knees, raising her torso slightly from its folded position. That position would have made my lower back spasm for a week. "I guess I want a contest," Alicia said. "I don't want to make anyone feel bad. I just want them to prove they deserve to have me tied up for them."

I nodded slowly, digesting what she'd said. The noise from the speaker beside us had forced me even closer to her by now. She smelled of freesia. She'd really gone all out for this Ethan guy. Irrational jealousy flashed through my stomach. "You thought he might be the one."

"At the last party, he tied my chest to my feet. For a couple seconds, I thought I might not be able to escape." She looked downright dreamy. I rolled my eyes.

"A lot of tops would say you should stay tied up out of respect for them."

"How am I supposed to respect them if they can't keep me tied up?"

I laughed. "How can you have any pudding if you don't eat your meat?"

"This is serious, Kristi."

I took a deep breath. I'd always considered Alicia's eel problem as a sympathetic friend. For the first time, I allowed myself to think like a top. A tricky domme, because that's what I had to be. I didn't have anywhere near Ethan's rope skills. An idea sparked in my chest, mingled with desire I'd never admitted before. "You want to get tied up, right? You don't need Ethan for that."

She groaned. "No one wants to tie me anymore. They're all afraid of being embarrassed."

Alicia spat the last word out, and I gave her a look. "For good reason."

"Whatever. It's still true. Nobody wants to play with an eel. At least, not an eel they can't beat."

A little warning voice spoke up in the back of my head. I'd

decided long ago not to play with Alicia, pretty as she was. I liked being her friend, and I honestly didn't know how well I'd handle her ego challenges myself.

I told that warning voice to go to hell. The force of wicked-top inspiration had already begun to energize my body.

I stood abruptly, my spine already making the tiny adjustments that take me from ordinary woman to scary black-leather-wearing domme. I nudged my rope bag with my boot and nodded toward my hands. I wriggled my fingers.

Alicia arched her eyebrow, her expression an elegant mix of invitation and skepticism. "Really."

Ten minutes later, we'd claimed a corner at the play party. With bundles of rope stacked up around me, I sat on Alicia's chest and examined her body with an architectural eye. Where to start?

Alicia squirmed under me. "Um, Kristi?"

"Yeah."

"You know I'm going to do the same thing I always do, right? I'm not going easy on you."

"I don't want you to go easy on me." I cracked my knuckles.

Her face screwed up into a miserable expression. "That's what people always say."

"Honey, I really know you. I know what you're capable of. I wouldn't be doing this if I hadn't accepted the possibility that you'll embarrass me by making it look like I didn't even remember to use knots." That wasn't strictly true. I had no intention of being embarrassed. I tried not to make the obvious comparisons to Alicia's macho boyfriends.

She relaxed only slightly. "Are you sure? I don't mean to be insulting, but you're not exactly…"

I let her feel a little more of my weight. "Give it to me, Alicia. I promise I'm good for it."

"Okay…" She still sounded doubtful. I reached for the fifty-foot length of hemp I like to use to lay my foundation.

I never got to it, because she slid out from under my legs in one smooth, muscular surge. I didn't hesitate. No need to find out how far she could and would run. Before she could go anywhere, I lunged at her football-player style, taking her down with a shoulder to her thigh.

She grunted, but rolled through the fall with practiced grace. I reached under her body and grabbed the back of her bra. It wasn't a chest harness, but it would do for a few seconds.

She bared her teeth and made it difficult for me, her body whipping and rolling from side to side. I threw myself across her, using my size against her as much as I could. I wouldn't have put it past her to bite, so I shifted my grip from her bra strap to her hair, snatching a fistful close to the scalp and keeping her head close to the floor and away from me.

I needed to get rope on her quickly, before she got the chance to demonstrate her superior martial arts skills. With no time to plan or select the perfect length of rope, I reached out blindly for the closest available. It turned out to be a thin silver nylon fifteen, which I normally used to add a metallic sheen to decorative chest harnesses.

Alicia thrashed like a demon beneath me. I couldn't afford to reject that rope and look for another one. The jiujitsu instructor who taught us both always says that pressure makes a person's purest martial arts come out, the moves that have become part of her being. I trusted that adage and allowed my hands to move faster than my brain. In seconds, I secured a passable single-column tie to Alicia's wrist. To give her something to keep her busy, I tacked it to her ankle.

I had no illusions—I knew she'd be out of it in seconds. Still, using clean, simple ties, I might stay just ahead of her, enough to avoid having to wrestle her and lose.

I kept going, barely looking at the ropes I grabbed. I used only the most basic knots, the ones that had truly become second nature. I manhandled Alicia, flipping and spinning her to lay those ties down at odd angles that I hoped would buy me more precious time.

At some point, my heart began to pound for a different reason. As I worked to enclose her strong, flexible body, I became painfully aware of the sexy contradictions of Alicia. So delicate. So indomitable. Sweat dampening her long, luxurious hair. The powerful muscles of her dancer's body standing out from her slim, sleek limbs. The nipples of her small breasts hard and visible through the lace of her bra. The smell of effort and arousal rising from her body.

My clit became aware, too. I could feel it growing inside my leather pants. I wanted to put my dick on and take her as my own.

Alicia sensed the change, too. She told me so with her wide, exhilarated grin and the challenge of her eyes. I knew she'd never let me fuck her until I'd paid my dues. She had to decide I'd earned it.

I'd never felt so determined.

I tied off my latest rope, satisfied for the moment by the web in which I'd trapped Alicia. She rocked gently on her stomach in a bow position, her arms pulled behind her and connected to her ankles with multiple layers of interwoven strands.

I'd done good work, especially considering the speed with which I'd had to tie her.

It wouldn't hold. The eel deserved her chance to play. I stepped out of her line of vision. If I was lucky, I'd have a couple of minutes now to try to convince my shoulders to unknot, and to get hold of the driving need in my cunt.

I made a show of organizing my pile of rope, palming that fifty-foot hemp in the process. Movement at the corner of my eye caught my attention. Round two had come already, and my breathing still hadn't returned to normal.

With no choice but to keep playing as hard as I could, I whirled, just in time to catch Alicia in the act of freeing herself from the last coil of my rope. Her disappointment at the ease of her escape was palpable. The moment of lethargy, however, gave me the opportunity I desperately needed.

Before she could get away, I dove for her, trapping her with my weight again. Alicia yelped in surprise. The sweaty, sweet smell of her slippery skin threatened to distract me. I wanted to lick her. Everywhere.

I still hadn't earned it.

This time, I started with the fifty, winding it around her torso as rapidly as I could. "Kristi, what the hell? I already proved your knots can't hold me."

I grinned down at her. "Honey, did you think I was only good for one shot? Those boys you're choosing must not have much stamina. I'm here all night." This, in fact, was my plan. If the sweat on her skin was any indication, she'd had to struggle to release herself, no matter how simple the challenge. Alicia might be more experienced at this game than I am, more flexible than I am and better at martial arts, but I had the rope on my side. I'd get rests, no matter how short. She wouldn't. At some point, I calculated, she'd be tired enough that I could lay down a good set of ties without having to fight her too hard. And I had some nasty tricks up my sleeve for when that moment came.

Her eyes widened with understanding. I'd shown my cards, but at this point I didn't think it would hurt my chances. "That's not fair!"

"Is that against the rules, sweetheart? I didn't know." I waited a beat, then continued. "You can safeword out if you don't like it. Otherwise, I'll tie you up over and over again until I teach you some respect." I punctuated the statement with an emphatic tug of the rope that made her sigh. Her body relaxed in my arms for just a second, and I caught a glimpse of the state Alicia craved but could not allow herself. The power of the vision made my hands tremble with desire.

I wound the rope around her chest a few more times, well aware that the more loops I added, the tighter my harness would feel. I couldn't help brushing her nipples in the process. I wanted to squeeze and suckle them. To concentrate on the task at hand, I promised myself that I could spend as long as I wanted on them once I took Alicia to the point of delicious surrender—a place I wasn't sure she'd actually been before. The idea of being the first top to take her there appealed to me with a fierce, primal tug. I guess everyone likes to pop a cherry.

This time, I tied her in the "damsel in distress" style, wrapping her in coils of rope from her upper arms down to her ankles. I hoped she'd have a slow, exhausting time ahead of her.

When I finished, I positioned her carefully on the floor. A lot of girls bliss out when they're lying inside a tight, restrictive tie. Not Alicia. The moment I released her, she started moving and twisting inside the coil, a small, determined smile playing over her lips.

This time I made no secret of watching her. The more I handled her, the hotter I got. I wanted to see her cute little body writhing on the floor at my feet. Besides, I needed to be responsible anyway and supervise her—might as well do that in a way I'd enjoy.

The rope undulated in response to Alicia's body. She stuck her tongue out of the corner of her mouth in concentration, seemingly oblivious to everything except the challenge at hand. I didn't take this personally. It was my rope that held her, after all. My ties. By focusing on that, she effectively focused on me.

I'd tied her as tightly as I could, and for several minutes she struggled without finding an opening. I couldn't help wondering what was going on inside the rope. Was her pussy juicing up in there? Was she getting off on the burn of the rope across her mostly naked body?

Alicia panted and threw her head back, her eyelids most of the way down. She certainly seemed to be having a sensual experience inside that coil. Again, I had to resist touching her. Even if I were willing to bend the rules of the game to my advantage, I wouldn't violate the sacred code underlying our contest. She'd made it clear she wouldn't grant respect until I proved I could hold her. And I wasn't about to ask for any favors until I had her respect.

The point of her knee emerged from between two loops of rope. She gave her right leg a funny wiggle, then drew her foot up inside the coil of rope. The toes of her right foot emerged a moment later, working at the tie around her left foot, loosening it steadily. They moved with the sort of subtlety and dexterity that most people have trouble achieving with their fingers. In another part of the coil, I caught a flash of Alicia's elbows, then the heels of her palms.

Like a butterfly, she wriggled and climbed her way out of my rope, slowly emerging in all her flushed, slick, beautiful glory. I couldn't have taken my eyes off her if I'd wanted to.

And I didn't feel embarrassed. The muscular artistry of Alicia's escape mesmerized me too much for that. I started to realize something that Alicia's other tops must have missed. For all her defiance, I still controlled her as she wrestled with my rope. The dance of emergence and transformation in front of me at that moment took a much different form than her escape from my single-column ties a few minutes before. It had its own shape and character, distinct also from the way she'd moved inside Ethan's ties.

Even though she wouldn't surrender to my rope, she'd still allowed me to place a claim on her. It was dynamic, being negotiated by her body before my eyes, but it was a claim nonetheless. She'd trusted and respected me that far, anyway.

Affection surged through me, and my plans changed just the slightest bit.

But I couldn't afford to bask in the glow of my discoveries, because Alicia had nearly finished freeing herself. I rocketed into action, my ties this time rough and nasty. I bent her like a pretzel, because I knew I could. I collapsed her body into a tight little ball in a modified version of a position the ancient Japanese used for interrogation.

She sighed and moved with me in a complex push and pull, a point and counterpoint of balanced strength. We could have been dancing. I felt impossibly graceful as we rolled together on the floor of the play party.

When I completed the tie, I spent a moment lying across her back, savoring the play of energy that flowed from me to her, from her to me, through the rope, then back again. Then I stood and stepped back, giving her room to play with me, the action no less electrifying for all that it occurred by proxy.

I glanced up and saw we'd attracted a crowd. I recognized several of the tops who'd played with Alicia in the past, but they showed no sign of the schadenfreude I'd expected. Instead, I picked up a few respectful nods and more than a little awe.

I couldn't let that pull me off my game. I dropped into a squat and focused on Alicia. Our connection had grown so that I could have sworn I felt her through the rope, even from several feet away. I knew just what it would feel like to grip her lathered sides. I knew the rhythm of her breath, her heart, the tense-and-release of her muscles. I knew exactly how tired she was, could see it in the little trembles that passed down her body.

Then she executed a double-jointed roll that seemed to turn her arms inside out. I blinked, amazed, as her improbable position allowed for dozens of little adjustments that made it possible for her to walk out of the balanced tension of a tie designed for an ordinary person.

Before she could get away, I wrapped her in my arms, cradled her against my chest. Restless little twitches still passed through her. I needed to go through one last round of our game. It was time to send the message I had in mind.

Alicia barely resisted when I wrestled her to the floor once more. This time, I employed the best tricks I could imagine. I took care to immobilize each of her joints, blocking her in all the places where she might begin to wriggle out. I assumed an insane range of motion. I took no tie for granted.

Then I anchored her feet in a flexed position and restrained each toe individually with little loops of paracord. I tied her left hand behind her back, then bent her palm back and tied her fingers to her wrist one by one.

Never had I tied so artfully, so thoroughly, so creatively. I wanted her to know everything I was capable of. But I didn't want to break her spirit. Not anymore. So I completed my treatment of her left hand, then stepped away deliberately, leaving her right arm entirely free of rope.

Alicia blinked and met my eyes. We looked into each other for a long time, and the rest of the world disappeared. I could have sworn the room went silent, though I don't think the music actually stopped.

I think we both understood something then because, ever so slowly, she tucked her right hand into position beside her left and bent her fingers as far toward her wrist as she could without assistance.

Maybe people clapped. I didn't care. I didn't look at anything but Alicia, submitting herself to me because she wanted to, because I'd earned her respect by respecting the beauty of her unconquerable flexibility.

I sat on the floor and pulled her bound body into my lap, so hungry for her that for a moment I wasn't capable of anything but holding her. Then I kissed her long and soft, savoring the slow-burning fire she returned. Her strength met mine, intact but muted. Her muscles quivered in my grasp, inside the web of my rope.

A few small adjustments, and I tugged the lacy bra away from her nipples. I stroked them softly at first, then got greedy. I pinched them hard, then grabbed her breasts in the palms of my hands and twisted and squeezed. She gasped, but her right arm never even twitched out of place.

I slid one hand under her body and offered it to her clit. Her thighs were wet and sticky. She'd soaked through her panties. Despite her obvious excitement, I'd bound Alicia so effectively that she couldn't grind against my hand. She whimpered in the back of her throat, but still didn't move to break out of my ties.

I released her instead, unknotting slowly, loop by loop. A little freedom for the hips. A little less tension on the feet. Another kiss, then more bend for the knee and less for the wrists.

At last, she was naked of rope. I gazed at my slippery little eel. She wriggled in my lap, rubbing her clit against my hand until she came.

NO STRINGS ATTACHED

James McArthur

I grasp the ends of the rope, nylon weave squeaking against my sweating fingertips. My shoulders ache and the coffee table is hard beneath my spine. My cock is throbbing inside my tight briefs. So many nights' fantasies are at play in my mind, I almost don't realize Graham is talking to me.

He grips my chin and makes me meet his gaze, shaking the images from my mind. "Nick, are you with me?" He told me not to speak without permission. Does asking a direct question confer permission? I don't know. I don't know the rules. But I want to learn them. I want Graham to teach me them. I stay quiet. "Good boy," he says. "I want you to keep a tight hold of that rope. It's only looped around your wrists loosely, but I've made it short enough to give you some tension. How do you feel?"

Do I speak? My answer would be too big for my mouth. I feel fuzzy in the head, weak at the knees, short of breath, hot and cold. I don't even know if Graham appreciates every little subtlety of the situation that's got me like this. Helpless against my body's craving. The fact that I've got my coveralls rolled right down to my hips and no top on and he's openly assessing my chest and abs, while he is still fully clothed. The fact that he's looming over me, his fingers still pressed into my jaw while I lie here completely immobilized. Not by the rope, which is more symbolic than effective, but by my lust and the fact that Graham is promising to make my long-held but unfulfilled fantasies real.

It's not what I'm expecting when I come in at eight for the night shift at George Saunders and Co. Polymer Products. Ted's name is on the roster. A good laugh is old Ted. But totty, he is not. I'm both pleased and apprehensive when Graham arrives and explains he's done a swap to let Ted get away on holiday. Pleased because Graham is totty. He knows he's hot and yet somehow pulls off the right level of affable cheek to make that okay. I'm apprehensive because we've flirted gently on the day shift since Graham started at the firm a month ago, but I don't know how to approach a twelve-hour stretch of the two of us alone on the plant. Twelve hours is a long time to spend with someone if they knock back your suggestion of a date.

"Hey, Nick, afraid you're stuck with me for the night," he grins as he walks in. I feign annoyance and the banter begins. Within minutes, we seem to be discussing our sex lives. "Got laid recently?" he asks.

"No, not since I broke up with my ex three months ago. I haven't felt like going out." I haven't felt like going out because my ex's complete rejection of my suggestion we try something new, something mildly kinky in the bedroom, flattened my confidence and left me feeling like some kind of freak. "What about you?"

"Met a nice-looking guy over the weekend. Yeah, we went back to his place, but I think it was just a one-off. I'm getting a bit fed up with one-night stands, to be honest. You can't have the best kind of sex unless you know someone well enough to really trust them, can you? How long were you with your ex?"

"Just over a year. Longest relationship I've had since my teens. I was with a schoolmate back then, but we drifted apart when he went to college."

"I was with someone for three years once, in my early twenties. But he went off traveling. It wasn't for me. I needed to be earning."

We watch the dials, noting down pressure and temperature readings every thirty minutes. Our boss is suspicious of technology. That's why we're here, working the night shift when the whole factory could be controlled by computers.

"We could go out for a drink sometime," I say, finally finding my courage around two.

"Yeah, we could." Instant relief that he hasn't said no. And that pelvic tingle that comes with the excitement of the new and unknown.

"So, why did you split with your ex?" he asks.

"Oh, you know, personal stuff."

"Personal sex stuff?"

"Yeah, kinda."

"Like what?"

He won't let it go. I excuse myself for a bathroom visit, tap the dials, make us coffee, offer cookies, flick through the logbook. Graham takes the book gently from my hands, closes it, puts it down, then takes my wrists and holds them firmly while he asks again, mouth close to my ear, "Like what?"

I start to think that he can sense my freakery in me. But he's holding my wrists tight, and I don't want to twist them away. I want him to back me into the control console. Which is what he does. And then he moves in and kisses me. I end up leaning back over the instrument panel uncomfortably. He keeps pushing with his lips, kissing me hard, his tongue rigid as it enters my mouth. But at the same time, he's holding me to him by my raised wrists. I can't straighten up and I can't collapse back and my abs are starting to shake. And it feels so good to be controlled. Held where he wants me. It's like he knows.

"Like what?" He whispers the words into my ear, his breath making me shiver. He doesn't let me move and I can feel his cock hardening against my stomach. My own is already stiff.

"I just, er. I just. Asked him if he'd mind me getting some handcuffs. Or if he could tie me to the bedposts."

It's easier to say because at that moment I'm staring intently at a freckle on the side of his neck rather than into his face. But when I'm done he pulls back, and I have to meet his gaze. "I knew it," he says. "I knew you were a kinkster." I think he might have actually pumped the air in triumph if he hadn't been holding my arms.

"I'm not..." I can barely say the word he's used, even though he said it so casually. "I'm not a 'kinkster.' I've never done anything like that before. I just thought we should try it. I wanted to know what it would feel like. I thought he might understand."

"And what did he say?"

I remember the words exactly. "He said, 'I'm not into that sort of thing.'" They seem so simple. But there was an underlying tone to them that said "that sort of thing" is wrong and you were wrong to say it instead of keeping it buried deep.

"Doesn't know what he's missing," Graham says. "Or maybe he does, but he's too ashamed to admit it. I bet that's it. Why else would he slap you down so fast?"

He looks at me until I feel I must be tomato red and want to just shrink through the floor. I'm wondering if his use of the word "slap" is as careless as his tone suggests. Then he says, "Do you still want to be tied up?"

Yes. I think about it every night, in the shower every morning, in the car on every commute, every time I jerk off. I look up sites on my laptop that make me feel like I'm going to be hauled from my bed at dawn by the perversion police. I browse handcuffs and rope at online sex shops but am too terrified of the package falling open in the delivery man's hands to ever order anything. "Yes," I say. "By the right man."

Graham clearly thinks he is the right man, without question. Which is what gets me here. Tied to the coffee table in the rest area in the back corner of the control room. Or, not tied, if we're being accurate. Blue nylon rope looped loosely around my wrists and grasped in my fists. It's one of those tables with a shelf underneath for magazines. The rope passes beneath that, pulling my arms down toward the floor. That's what makes my shoulders ache.

"I can't exactly hog-tie you right here," he says, while I'm still backed up to the control panel. "Not very safe if something on the plant overheats. Wasn't there an emergency shutdown last week?" The word "hog-tie" sounds so dirty and demeaning to my novice ears, it makes me gasp. Or maybe it's a groan.

"Yes, Wednesday. Fire department was here and everything. A valve had got stuck."

"Hmm. Fire department, you say?" He winks and steps back, letting go of my wrists. I shift my butt from where it has become molded around the edge of the control panel. "Only joking," he says. "I wouldn't really hog-tie you on the factory floor and then call the fire department. Not tonight." He grins like he might actually do it another night. I'm reminded, however comically, that I don't really know this guy.

"But I'm sure we could do something to give you a taster.

Without actually inhibiting your freedom in the event of an emergency. I hate to see you suffering like this. How about it?"

It's not just about safety in the factory. It's like he knows what I'm thinking and he's giving me a way to try this, where it doesn't matter that I don't know him very well. It's just a taster, a trial run, no strings attached. Something to ease my suffering, which is a pretty upside-down way of putting it.

"Okay," I say, very quietly. He grins like a schoolboy.

"Sit there," he says, pointing to the low table, its wood-effect plastic laminate worn at the edges where decades of boots have rested on it. "I'm improvising here, so bear with me. How would you feel about putting your hands on your head while I go on recon for supplies?"

"Um, okay." I think that if that's the only response required of me, I'll cope, but I really don't think I can formulate any full sentences right now. I sit on the table and start to raise my arms. "Oh, and you might as well take your coveralls down to your waist and get your top off, too."

I do it, fingers fumbling with the zip front of the dark blue canvas work-wear. I roll them down to my hips, just like I do at the end of every shift in the locker room. I pull off my T-shirt, dropping it on the threadbare couch. He's looking in the janitor's cupboard to the side of me. I raise my arms, linking my fingers on my head, flattening my hair. If I'd known Graham was going to be on the night shift I'd have gelled it. But now I realize it's good I didn't because my hands are damp with sweat and I'd only mess it up. I stare straight ahead at the gray controls and the window that looks down on the works. For some reason, it seems the thing to do. Eyes front, like it's an army inspection or something. I hear him making little noises of delight. "Oh yes, perfect." "Ooh, this is interesting." Then he's in front of me, with a blue rope, a roll of duct tape and a broom in his hands.

My mouth falls open, and my eyes widen in a way that I thought only happened in cartoons.

"Ha!" He's bursting with glee. "Got you. I'm only kidding with the broom. I just wanted to see the look on your face. We'll save that for another time, when I've broken you in a bit more."

Oh my fucking god. He's teasing me and my cock is rock hard and horribly constricted in my underwear. He looks down at me with those cute blue eyes. He has the sort of eyes that will always make him look sweet in spite of his shaved head and unkempt stubble.

"I'm just going to use this." He holds up the rope. It's that kind of blue, half-inch synthetic stuff you find lying around in factory stores but which has no known purpose.

"Okay," I say.

"Oh, I forgot to tell you not to speak. My mistake. No more talking, sweet cheeks." He bends down and puts a finger on my lips, affecting a solemn demeanor. I try to slow my breathing to make it look like I might still be in control of my bodily responses. Graham kneels in front of me and shows me what he'll do with the rope. He measures it against the width of the table and puts two wide loops in it to go at either side. He tells me—orders me, I guess—to turn around and lie back. I feel just the slightest touch of his fingers as he slips the loops onto my wrists.

I want more than the slightest touch. I want his hands all over me and, of course, he knows this. He places the roll of duct tape on my bare abdomen, raising a thousand and one images in my mind of what he could do with it. I don't answer his question, "How does it feel?" I keep my lips closed, imagining what it would feel like to have them taped shut.

Graham lets go of my chin after the question and runs his hands over my chest and down my stomach, around the roll of tape, stopping short at the top of my briefs. My back arches to meet his touch and the tape wobbles. For some reason, I suddenly find it an important goal to keep the tape in place.

"Tut tut," he says. "You'll have to learn more discipline than that." The word makes my throat tighten. He grasps one of my ankles and presses it to the leg of the table. "If I could, I would tie your ankles down, too." I voluntarily press the other leg into the opposite side. "I would have you completely naked." He walks his hands up my legs, thumbs pressing into my inner thighs, and onward, stopping just beneath my tight balls. "Except, maybe, for a butt plug."

I have to swallow; my mouth is swimming in saliva. I stare at the polystyrene-tiled ceiling, breathing hard, until Graham rubs the heel of his hand over my trapped dick. Then, I lift my head and look at him. It doesn't go unnoticed. He steps astride the table, rising over me, and bends to put a hand around my neck. My brain tells me I should be shocked and frightened. But he rests his hand around my throat so gently I register nothing but desire. "And if you're going to do that, I could collar you. I have a steel one. Imagine if it was fixed down to the table, pinning your neck in place." I can feel the cold metal on my skin, the restriction against my airway.

"Fuck," I gasp, breaking the rules. "You have a steel collar? Do you do this a lot then?"

He sinks down until he's sitting on my pelvis, my cock crushed and throbbing beneath his balls. He's a big guy and the weight makes me tense muscles I didn't know I had down there to stop him from squashing me.

"I don't remember allowing you to speak, but since you did, yes, I've done this before." He keeps the pressure on my throat light, but moves his thumb and forefinger up to my jawbone so I can't move my head. When he puts the palm of his other hand across my mouth, I have an urge to lick it. "But I'd forgotten what it's like to be a novice with a world of possibilities ahead of you." He makes it sound like a magical wonderland. "I've always loved being tied up. But it took me a while to discover how much I enjoy giving other guys that feeling. And you, a newbie. You're so responsive. I want to spend a long time with you finding out what you like. There's so much to try." He's like a kid in a sweetshop.

I realize I've managed to part my lips beneath his palm and am flicking my tongue onto his sweat-salted skin.

"I should tape your mouth to stop you doing that," he says. "But just imagine having to pull the tape off quick if the fire alarm sounds. Ouch." My hips are rocking beneath him and if he keeps talking like this I might actually come from the slightest friction of my briefs. The rope is cutting into my wrists, because I'm grasping it so tightly.

"You have a lovely body. I'd like to cover it with rope marks. And you mentioned handcuffs." I moan a little. "But right now, I have to go and take the three a.m. readings. Don't move."

I feel too light, too free, with his weight gone from my pelvis and his hands gone from my face and neck. I press my legs into the sides of the table and imagine that collar pinning my head into my place. I imagine rope wound all around my body so tight I can't budge an inch. I imagine tape across my mouth and a blindfold over my eyes. I imagine Graham bending me over first to push a fat butt plug inside me. I'm well away with this very detailed fantasy when I realize he's finished doing the readings and is standing just out of my line of sight looking at me as my hips pulse and my chest heaves. I glance up and see him raise his eyebrows.

"You are going to be such fun," he says. "You're not working tomorrow night, are you?"

I shake my head.

"I guess we could still meet for a drink," he says. "But we'd have more time to play if you come straight over to my place. Agreed?"

I nod.

ROPING THE COWBOY

Teresa Noelle Roberts

"Have you ever tied up a cowboy, ma'am? Because I'm available if you'd like to."

I turned to the man who'd just propositioned me, ready to snarl at him.

Instead, I smiled.

I live in a city with the unofficial motto "Keep Austin Weird," so I'm inured to oddity. And since I'm a pretty woman with flame-patterned hair and a fondness for wearing Docs with fishnets and very short skirts, I sometimes get hit on in fairly outrageous ways.

Which is fine if the outrageous come-on is also polite. Hell, if the polite outrageous line is being delivered by someone hot, I'm not above considering it. And the guy asking the provocative question was a tall, handsome, dark-haired example of one-hundred-percent-genuine cowboy.

You see a lot of desk jockeys in Stetsons and boots around here—this is the capital of Texas, after all, even if Austin is more known for tech and alternative music than cattle these days. But I can pick a real cowboy among the wannabes by the way he carries himself (or herself—there are real cowgirls, too), the way he wears his hat, a weathered, wind- and sun-burned look and fine crow's feet, even if he's young. But mostly it's the eyes. Cowboys are used to a long focus, looking at a far horizon, not at a computer. So when a cowboy chooses to focus on you, it *is* a choice and he really focuses, like you matter, not like you just happen to be in his line of vision. This particular cowboy was focusing his greenish-brown eyes, and his attention, on me in a way I'm not used to seeing in someone I *don't* have tied up already. Like I was the gateway to a heaven he never thought he'd reach.

And did I mention handsome? Cheekbones to die for, a deep tan and dark hair, almost black, with a few featherings of silver. Broad shoulders. Narrow hips. His intense hazel eyes were almond-shaped and fringed with long lashes like a showgirl's, an arresting note of softness in his knife-edge appearance.

"What makes you think I'd want to tie up a cowboy, cowboy?" I raised the bourbon I'd been nursing to my lips and looked into his eyes as I sipped. His eyes narrowed but his pupils dilated. He leaned toward me, but stopped before he got into my personal space. I swear I felt his dick harden.

It was hard to tell in the bar light, especially with his dark complexion, but I swear he flushed. "Right before they went to the restroom, your friends were teasing you about boys and rope. Sorry for eavesdropping."

When Heather and Dana are tipsy, you don't need to eavesdrop. They make sure everyone knows whatever they're oversharing. Sometimes this was an annoyance. Tonight, I'd call it a feature.

I swung my legs around to the side, making sure he got a good look at the fishnets, and at everything my little red dress wasn't hiding. "It's fun to tie up boys. But it's more fun to tie up men." I looked at him as coolly as I could, smiling a slow, predatory, red-lipped smile. "Which are you, cowboy?"

He gulped and glanced away. His big hand fumbled with his empty beer bottle. But when he looked back at me, his gaze was steady. "Like to think I'm a man. But I reckon I'll be whichever you want tonight. That is, if you're interested."

"Good answer. Next question: do you always ask strange women to tie you up?"

"Never." Something in his voice told me he was telling the truth. "I've always been curious, but never knew how to ask. Can't ask a woman who knows me well, because she thinks I'm one kind of man and might get turned off finding out I don't always want to be the tough guy. Can't ask a stranger because it's a good way to get slapped. Thanks to your friends and their pink drinks, I know you like bondage. And I'm hardly ever in Austin, so if I make a fool of myself we'll never see each other again. Figured you'd probably say no, but you probably wouldn't slap me." He stopped and looked stunned, as if he didn't know where all the words had come from.

I set my drink down and leaned in toward him. "What makes you think I was going to say no?"

Then I kissed him. My hands went to his wrists, holding them, and while it was obvious my small hands could only immobilize him if he chose to obey me, he did.

I paid the bar tab—my friends' too, because I owed them a thank-you—as I hastily explained when they returned from the restroom to find me kissing a cowboy. My new chew toy, Jake, followed me home, driving an F450 that had clearly seen heavy use.

We went through some quick negotiations, which I think surprised Jake pleasantly. I don't think it had occurred to him

agony of the cold/hot feeling spreading through me seems over-whelming. Yet, somehow, I pull on my reserve of strength, regulate my breathing and still my body. "Good girl." I can hear the smile in his voice. I know I made him proud. That in itself is enough to spread some heat in my frozen places. "Don't move," he admonishes. I lock my limbs in place and wait and wait. Sweat starts to trickle down my spine and pool in the crease of my knees. I feel my muscles burn from the strain of keeping still. Just when I think I can't take it anymore, I hear movement on my right side. I sigh.

Van's warm fingers caress every inch of my skin that is not covered by the jute ropes. They reach the toppled candle and steady it back on my navel. His right hand, dripping in hot, oily wax, travels back up my torso. The fiery shock jolts my nipples erect even more. The blazing heat is spread around my breasts as the satiny hand kneads my tender flesh. I feel my cheeks flush. My blood is reaching its boiling point. The storm brewing inside crests; I feel it so close to the peak. "Oh, no, you don't," he smirks.

Out of nowhere his left hand is on my thigh, the tip of the cocksicle is pressing against my opening. I don't think I can take this cold/hot invasion again. Before I can decide if I truly can, Van is sliding the cocksicle up and down my labia, teasing my clit with its icy tip. My hips buck. "Be still," he commands. His right hand travels south, picks up the candle, tips it down. The sting of the oily wax hitting my clitoris, even if anticipated, is a shocking contrast.

The hand moves away with the candle, leaving a scorching trail from my pubic bone to my nipples. "Ow," I cry out when the hot liquid hits my frozen pebbles. Van doesn't give me time to adjust. With a flick of his wrist, the cocksicle is plunged deep inside my vagina. His fingers pluck and pull my nipples while his other hand pushes and pulls the ice dildo in and out of my velvet walls and folds in a fast, furious motion.

His hot breath is on my neck as he sucks back air in ragged pulls. His fingers don't cease their delicious erotic attack. The cocksicle is melting inside my wet heat. I feel it disintegrating inch by inch. The cold/hot tug-of-war surging through me ends abruptly. All of a sudden, my body is one colossal lava ball ready to explode. All I want is that sweet, sweet release that only he can give me. I am so close. The words are on my lips. I don't have time to utter them.

In one swift move the suspension cord holding me in place drops a few inches; the ice dildo is wrenched out of me, my body is tilted, crushed against a naked, hard, hot torso; his lips fuse to mine and in one thrust he's there, filling, stretching and claiming me.

There's nothing melting about his cock. It's fully erect and thick, and erotically stroking every inch of me, including that incredible spot that makes my eyes roll toward the back of my head. The storm cresting inside rips out of me in a torrent. "Give it to me, *kisâ*. Now." His words release the flood. "Damn, Tatem, you're so hot. So fucking hot," he groans against my lips as his cock keeps plunging deeper and deeper inside my molten core.

His fingers trail between our bodies and reach my clit. They circle it. Flick it. Press it. Hard and fast they work it. Under his agile ministrations, it sings to a new rhythm. To my complete disbelief, I feel that ball of lava tugging in my lower abdomen again. His mouth breaks away from mine, kisses my throat, licking, nibbling and sucking along the way. My breathing shallows. His lips trace my left clavicle, then the right one, before he dips down to claim my puckered nipples one at a time.

The lava ball expands and expands. His cock is pummeling

my vagina in a most luscious way. His fingers keep worshipping my clit and the way his mouth and tongue are revering my nipples is heavenly. No wonder I am on the edge again. "Give me more, *kisâ*." The need in his voice is my undoing. I fall. Fall. Fall.

In the midst of my erotic free fall I register the feel of Van's arm slipping underneath my neck. He nestles my head in the crook of his elbow. The ripple of his bicep against my cheek increases my coital bliss. I am light and free. Like a feather dancing in the wind, landing on the soft, heated wooden planks of the floor.

"Hey beautiful, come back to me." He nuzzles his nose behind my earlobe and gently coaxes me back to earth. His nimble fingers start to unknot my right ankle. I feel a warm salve being applied to the red blistering circles. His long digits work in the healing balm all around my ankle and continue their enchanting journey up my calf, knee, kneading muscles, getting the blood circulating again. Up and up my thigh they go, round and round my hip, until they reach my backside. They stop their nurturing to work out the knots and free my right wrist. The same warm healing salve is applied to the red marks encircling the limb.

I love the feel of Van's fingers on my skin. Strong. Skillful. Patient. They knead and roll my muscles, working some life back into them. They graze over my sensitized nipples, and I moan. Van gives them each a small tweak and continues to massage and unknot the jute ropes holding me in place. His fingers are now moving down my left side; their goal is clear as they ply apart the knot holding my wrist captive. Once it's freed from its bond, Van applies more of the heavenly balm.

"You're doing so well, *kisâ*. Hold on just a bit more," he coos as his digits begin to undo the last knot holding my ankle in place. They make short order of it and soon the warm creamy mixture is applied and massaged deep in my tissues all the way to my toes. I feel the blood surging in my ears as it rushes down to my lower limbs.

Van scoops me up in his arms and carries me across the floor, down the flight of stairs, through an open doorway and settles me down on the ceramic tiles of the master bathroom. I hear him remove his pants, the black drawstring yoga ones, faded and soft from over-washing. The only article of clothing he ever wears when we play. I feel a pang of disappointment that he didn't remove my blindfold before stripping out of them. The way they hang off his hips makes my blood race and my mouth water. Just imagining them on his long sculpted legs and lean waist makes my breath shallow.

His arms wrap around my waist. His hands come up to cup my breasts. "You're all slippery," he whispers. I arch my back and lean into his caress. "Greedy little minx," he teases and swats my behind in a playful manner. "Let's get you cleaned up." He guides me inside the shower stall and only when the hot water is cascading down on us does he remove my blindfold.

"Hi," he murmurs.

"Hi," I whisper back.

His lips capture mine and I am lost in the sensation of him, his expert tongue tasting, drinking. Like a man who's discovered water in the middle of a desert, he can't seem to get enough of the nectar my mouth has to offer. His hands dip in my hair, coiling around the long strands, tilting my head back against the cool ceramic walls. At this angle his tongue plunges deeper inside, exploring the darker, richer fare; he doesn't find it wanting. Our hot breath mixing together is enough to sustain me as I let him pull me into this endless soul-searing kiss.

"Tatem, I'll never get enough of you," he breathes in my mouth as he slams into me. My legs lift off the shower floor and wrap around his waist. My hands lock behind his neck, my fingers twirling and pulling his wiry black hair. To tease and torture me, he quickly pulls out. "Please," I cry.

This time Van's movements are languorous, delicious. I feel him caress my inner walls as he pushes himself inch by inch inside of me. He tilts his pelvis upward. His infamous curve dips against my spongy spot. Again and again he slips out and inches back in. Stroking, caressing me, *there*, on that feel-so-good spot, but just when I think he'll pick up the pace, press into me hard and make me convulse, he slows, hovers, slips out and starts the tantalizing dance all over again.

Under the beating pelt of the shower, I am sweating. My limbs feel like Jell-O. His mouth is still on mine. His tongue hasn't ceased its exploration of every nook and crevice of my mouth. I relish its invasion. I meet him twist for twist, caress for caress. My nipples are hard, elongated and taut. I press them against his rippling chest. They scrape on his coarse hair. The tingly feeling it evokes travels from the crested tip straight to my groin. My clitoris pulses to the rhythm of Van's strokes; slowly in, slower out, slowly in, slower out. The friction this creates is erotic as hell, but I am not sure how much more I can bear. I feel that ball of lava again rapidly growing in the pit of my stomach.

"You feel so good." His voice is tight, full of need.

"So do you," I say in my own breathless voice.

"Open your eyes. I want to watch you watch me."

I keep my eyes on his lovely face as he keeps up the antagonizingly slow speed of his thrusts. "This is what you to do me," he rasps against my lips. And then he's flying, pounding me like a demon. The thump, thump, thump of my ass hitting the tiles makes my heart rate dance to the same beat. I feel him expand inside of me. He tilts his pelvis and he's *there*, pressing his engorged head hard against my sweet sensitive spot. My eyes roll back. "Look at me, Tatem." I try to focus my sight on him. "Yes," he screams, and finds his release.

I detonate around him, squeezing him deeper inside of me, milking more of his erotic juice. "And this is what you do to me," I say, and slump against him. He slides us down to the shower floor. I sit on his lap with him still buried inside of me. We rock gently back and forth, cradling each other's bodies.

"Say it again."

I know it cost him a great deal to ask. My heart swells in my chest. Here is my burly man, asking for reassurance. "I'll miss you," I whisper above his heart and plant a kiss over the thumping organ. His arms tighten around me. I feel his smile against my cheek. I lift my eyes up to his. The look he gives me is full of mischief and mystery. "What?" I ask.

"Come." He pulls us up, slipping out of me, and starts to wash my body and shampoo my hair. His fingers make quick work of the tasks and soon he's wrapping me in a white fluffy towel. "Come," he says again.

Van guides me into the master bedroom. He keeps his eyes locked on mine, runs his long sexy fingers in his hair, exhales a deep breath and asks, "How much will you miss me, Tatem?"

My mind is on overdrive. *Where is he going with this?* My breathing accelerates from the thrill of not knowing. My mouth goes dry. I try to speak but no sound comes out. I swallow what little saliva I manage to produce and try again. "A lot."

"Good."

My eyebrow arches.

"So, a lot you say."

I nod my head, unable to produce any more saliva to wet my throat.

"Would you say that you'd miss me so much, that when you

think of me you'll want to touch yourself?" His voice is soft. Too soft.

My heart is slamming against my rib cage. My palms are cold and moist.

"Answer me, Tatem." Again his voice is too soft.

I am weary. He normally uses that tone when I've been naughty and need punishing. Today wasn't supposed to be about punishment, only pleasure. This was our special treat before I leave for the plains for two and half weeks, to launch my new eco-friendly brand of cosmetics and other beauty accessories. Once again my mind is reeling, wondering where he's going with this.

"Tatem!"

I bite my lip hard. Swallow once. And respond. "Yes, Van, I would. Want to touch myself when I think about you."

"Good."

Relief floods over me as his tone takes on his natural timber.

"Close your eyes," he commands.

Without hesitation my eyelids come down. My long lashes tickle my cheeks.

"I have a present for you. Don't move."

I stay glued to the spot he's placed me in as my ears strain to hear him rummaging around the chest of drawers at the foot of the king-size bed. I hear the scrape of metal, the turn of a key, the dingle and dangle of objects as they clatter one against the other. A drawer is pulled open and closed. Van's footfall approaches and when he's in front of me, the air moves as he bends down. "Step." I lift my left foot off the floor and step inside a hoop. "Again." I lift my right foot and step inside another hoop.

The object is moved up my legs; the feel of the leather is a surprise as Van's fingers move it up and up and over my hips. I feel him tighten buckles and cinch me into place. I hear a small clink.

"Open."

My eyes flutter open and look down. My lips form a huge O.

Van chuckles and brings me into his arms to kiss my stunned lips. "From this day forward, Tatem, I want to be the only one to give you pleasure." He shows me the small key that will allow him just that and kisses me one more time.

"Miss Silverthorne?"

"Miss Silverthorne?"

A gentle hand is on my shoulder. I open my eyes and notice the tall blonde flight attendant bending over me.

"Yes,"

"I need to see your belt."

It takes me a nanosecond to realize that she means the seat belt and not the one hidden underneath my Chanel suit.

"Surely," I reply with a smile tugging on my lips. I lift my hands from my lap and show her that I am properly belted in.

PEGGED

Emily Bingham

"Do you trust me?" I ask, straddling his lap.

He looks at me from the dark pools of his eyes over the rim of his thick glasses, the hint of a shy grin on his lips. Slowly, he nods, almost as if it pains him to admit it. I take his curly head in my hands and lean in to kiss him. The boy is talented with his tongue, his mouth so inviting that at times it's easy to get lost in. Part of me wants to be greedy, roll over and let him have his way—splay me open and worship the folds between my legs as long as he likes.

I resist the urge, wanting tonight to be about him and taking him where he wants to go. It's his turn to be small and defenseless for an evening. I want to be so kind to him that it becomes cruel.

This game of taking control over such a sweet man, a gentle giant who dwarfs me in every way, amuses me each time we play it. Who am I to tell him what to do? His hand is big enough to engulf half my chest; with just the strength of one arm he could—and regularly does—toss me aside and take what he wants. We both know he could turn the tables at any time.

When my words lead the way, the unspoken promise he makes is to follow them, transporting him to a fantasy land where he is tiny yet powerful, and all mine. My promise is to use him comfortably within his boundaries, poking gently at what hasn't been explicitly asked for without ever crossing the line.

For the moment, we kiss as equals, with hands roaming the naked expanse of each other's bodies. My legs wrap around the girth of his waist, pulling him close to tease both of us with the proximity of his growing hardness to my pussy. It would only take me lifting my hips at the right angle to have him inside me. We join mouths ardently around the enticing hunger this knowledge creates, dancing around the possibility until it becomes too much to bear.

When I can't resist the urge any longer, I untangle myself from his body, stifling my sigh of frustration. I want to fuck him, and I hate that denying him means tormenting myself as well. In order to resist the compulsion, I stand while taking a deep breath. My knees are trembling, but I try not to give my longing away while looking at him. As I stand there teasing him with the sight of my naked body, he grins, not knowing what I have in mind. This thought makes me smile wickedly and arch an eyebrow at the predicament that unwinds in my mind. There's an expression he gets at loaded moments like this—somewhere between awe and skepticism—a wrinkle to his forehead that almost makes me want to take pity on him. Almost.

As my first act of cruelty, I take his glasses, leaving everything fuzzy at the edges and a bit more mysterious. It strikes me that so much of my mental image of him revolves around his eyewear, it's only without them that he seems truly naked. Keeping him at arm's length, I run my fingers through his hair, giving him time to contemplate his fate. Eyes closed and body pliable, he gives in to the simple pleasure of having his head stroked.

While he's unaware of what's about to unfold, I take the opportunity to whisper in the whorl of his ear, "Be a sweetheart and kneel on the bed." He does, with no reluctance, situating his handsome round behind in the air, wagging it subtly. I walk slowly to the bed. Rather than giving in to temptation by sticking my face in the furry mounds of his ass, I tease us both by reaching under the bed.

Knowing the sorts of objects that live in the darkness of this space, he tenses slightly but doesn't move away when I pull out a tangle of hemp rope. He offers me his wrists without being told. I bind them together in front of him, using a simple tie meant to remind him who's in control and keep his sneaky fingers at bay. With his hands bound securely, I kiss my way along his body, watching his ass dance in the air again, begging for attention. Unable to resist any longer, I run my fingers in a soft tickle over the furry thing he presents, enjoying the reaction this elicits.

"You think that's funny?" He stops mid-laugh to respond, but his words are stymied by my palm meeting his ass. The sound is shocking in the quiet of the room. I slap it again to ensure he's paying attention, his exaggerated whimpers exciting me. Before I can spank him again, he has the impudence to taunt me by wiggling his behind. "Look at that naughty thing!"

I raise my hand, liking the way he tenses his cheeks in anticipation. Rather than follow through with the implied threat, I slide onto the bed to prop myself against the headboard and slip my legs underneath him. This time when he shakes his ass defiantly, I grab hold and deposit him into my lap. Given our size difference, it's a fairly ridiculous situation; he isn't in my lap so much as I am trapped under his bulk. Luckily, we both have a sense of humor when it comes to these matters.

He isn't wiggling anymore, seeming to have been surprised into behaving. With him closer, it's easier to hold him still with one hand and spank him rhythmically with the other, watching his behind redden. The noises he makes verge on dissent, but the hard cock that presses into my leg lets me know he enjoys the predicament.

"Someone seems to be having fun." He raises his body to allow me to reach under him and gently take his cock in my hand. My palm is tender from the repeated sting of hitting him so that the smooth head of his member is like a balm to my tingling skin.

There is no disputing his erection, and yet he shakes his head. I laugh. "No?" He denies it again as I run my hand over his shaft, not giving him the luxury of any friction. "I don't believe you." He continues insisting to the contrary as I make my touch lighter, feeling his cockhead dance against me. "Then what is this?" I give it one good squeeze, enjoying his sigh and the disappointed noise that follows when I don't continue.

"Nothing." He mumbles, face buried in the sheets, bound hands clawing at the edge of the mattress to seek some kind of solace from my teasing.

"I don't believe that, either." I slap his behind with the hand that isn't tormenting him, the one he hadn't been paying any attention to. It surprises him enough that he looks at me over his shoulder with that lost puppy dog look, as if I've betrayed him. His pained expression opens up some part of me that wants to keep hurting him until he asks me to stop. I spank him several more times with one hand while the other just barely grazes the head of his cock.

I abruptly stop both actions. Feeling him so hard and

moaning while using nothing but my hands to torment him is going to my head. "Did I give you permission to enjoy this so much?" Burying his face farther into the bed, he says no wordlessly, and I'm surprised at how small he can seem when bound and chastised.

I spit into my hand to wet the inside of my thighs, pulling him into my lap so that his cock slides into the moist crevice I've made for him. "Now, if you're a good boy, I'll only have to give you ten more. But, if you keep this up," I squeeze his cock for emphasis, "I'll have to assume you aren't going to behave. Understand?"

He nods frantically and I can feel him using every fiber of willpower not to move his hips against the slippery place where I've trapped him. I wait to see if he can control himself. Only when he proves he can be still do I count aloud while applying the promised spanks. He does well until I get to the ninth firm slap to his already red behind. Just as I'm about to apply my hand the final time, I feel him buck against my thighs.

"Naughty!" I roll him off my lap so that his lovely hardness points in the air, looking so much like it's about to burst I almost take him in my mouth, wanting so badly to see him get off and to taste him on my tongue. Somehow I find the willpower to resist, wondering if he knows: how much I want him, how difficult it is to continue being cruel, that I would rather get fucked than punish him.

While standing, I notice that the wetness on my thighs is no longer simply saliva. He watches as I run a finger through this mess, shaking my head disapprovingly before placing the finger in my mouth to taste the sticky business he left behind. This causes him to raise his hips and suck in a sharp breath, wanting to ask for a taste but not daring.

I tsk my tongue at his continued inability to behave, as I

walk around the bed. "You naughty thing, you enjoyed that too much. We'll have to find another way to teach you to follow instructions."

His sweet face threatens to soften my resolve but I manage to stay strong, searching under the bed for more rope. This time I reach for thin cord, more akin to shoelace than anything useful for restraint. I crawl onto the bed to plant a thigh on either side of his face, holding my pussy purposefully just out of his reach, teasing him with the smell of what he can't have. "Don't you dare," I remind him. I don't even feign kindness as I kneel down closer to him. "See how wet hurting you makes me?"

A throaty and pathetic "Mm-hmm" passes his lips and I can tell he's barely able to keep his mouth to himself. Reaching across his body, I wrap the tiny rope around his dick, making a snug tailor-made cock ring, finished off with a dainty little bow. It looks so much like a lovingly wrapped present that I can't help leaning down to kiss the head sweetly just once. His moan makes me long to continue.

While he's distracted, I lower myself onto his mouth. "Okay, you can make me come now." He hesitates for only a moment before lapping at the wet folds of my pussy, his tongue not missing an inch, teasing and satisfying at equal turns, needing no instruction to bring me to the edge and back. He builds the electricity of my desire until it is a physical thrum in the room, making it nearly impossible to not grind myself into his face.

Even with his hands bound, he is able to reach far enough to grasp my ass, cupping it and squeezing. I want to ride the bliss of his tongue tickling me in the sweetest places as long as possible before giving myself over to it. He ruins all my plans of holding out by pushing my hips into his face and licking industriously at my clit. There is no way to pull away now as I ride the waves of endless orgasm, bucking against his face, grinding on his tongue as it flickers away, sending me over again and again. It's an endless loop that he can maintain as long as he wishes. As long as he touches me, the live wire he has exposed will keep coming. This is his present for being so patient.

When I've had enough, I lift myself away from his reach. I lean in and kiss his messy face, tangling tongues with him to taste my own tanginess on his lips before whispering, "Thank you; such a good boy you are."

I stroke his hair and caress his bearded face, reveling with him in this calm moment. As a treat I reach down to play with him, wetting my palm and rubbing it tenderly on the head of his bound cock until he is thrusting up into my hand, silently asking for more. Before he can get too invested in believing I'm finished with him, I stop.

"Do you want to be untied?" He shakes he head and looks at me coyly. "Naughty thing." I smile, pleased, and reach for several more coils of hemp rope, resting them on his chest so that he can enjoy the weight and earthy smell of them until I'm ready to put them to use.

First, I carefully slide his glasses over his ears so that he can watch as I secure his bound wrists to the headboard with one of the lengths of rope, anchoring him to the center of the bed. I lean down to kiss him deeply, tasting myself again on his eager tongue. When I am able to pull myself away, I nibble my way down his body, only barely resisting the urge to suck him off as I pass by his belly.

Grabbing his ankle, I guide it to bend his knee so that I can tie his ankle to his thigh in a frogged position. I wrap a long rope around the ankle and thigh followed by another line through that to secure it in place, applying the rope tenderly to contrast the tightness of the finished tie, which I tug to set the square knot in place. Repeating this tie on his other leg forces them to stay splayed apart, the rope keeping him from resting them on the bed. This exposes his cock and ass nicely.

As I look at how well secured he is, I notice him blush at the implications of how I've bound him. He watches with wide eyes as I buckle on my six-inch purple strap-on, tightening it around my waist and between my legs. "You're going to use that on me?" he asks.

"If you ask nicely."

His blush deepens as I lift myself onto the bed between his legs, so close that my rubber phallus touches his thigh, reminding him of its presence but not putting it to use quite yet. I tickle his thighs, enjoying watching him try to get them away from me even though they are so thoroughly bound. He laughs but doesn't speak. I raise my eyebrow at him as a reminder that I'm waiting for him before I can continue. When he still doesn't ask for what he wants, I decide to make it impossible for him to be silent, to tease him until he has to beg.

I lubricate one finger and use it to make lazy circles on his exposed asshole where it peeks out so demurely under his bound cock. He moans and tries to lean into my finger, which only motivates me to caress his opening even more slowly. His sounds of pleasure quickly become grunts of frustration.

"Can I help you?" He pouts but doesn't speak. "I can't give you what you want unless you tell me. Use your words." I watch his cock twitch at attention as I slowly penetrate his ass with my slippery finger, holding it very still inside him. "Is that what you want?"

He nods his head furiously. "So just the one finger then? All right." I begin twisting it around inside him, using a come-hither motion on his prostate, daring him to speak. All I get for my trouble is a frustrated grunt as he bucks his hips off the bed, trying to trick me into fucking him. "Oh, you want more?"

"Yes, please," he pleads. I place a second finger in him but don't move it either. He grunts and moves against me as best he can. "Please?"

"Please what?"

"Please...fuck me."

"Such a nice boy to ask." With my two fingers I begin penetrating him methodically, listening to him mumble nonsense. It isn't long before he tries in vain to get into any position where he can move himself against me, not fully understanding that with his legs tied as they are he can't get the leverage to do so.

"More." He begs.

I slip another finger in and continue my glacial pace. He still groans, appearing to be in more pain from this game than he ever was from the spanking. "Is that what you wanted?"

"No," he whimpers, and I remove my fingers. He widens his eyes, entreating and out of breath. His come is dribbling onto the pretty rope bow around the base of it, the sight of which makes me stroke my rubber cock, where he can see, luring him.

"Please? Oh, please." It comes out of him as a mantra, again and again, as if the teasing has left him only these words.

I continue fondling the strap-on, making it so slippery it gleams, refusing to give in. "Please, what?"

He looks helpless as he struggles to find the words, knowing what he wants but fighting with the notion of asking for such a filthy thing. As he works up the bravery to speak, he struggles against the rope, trying to get free. He looks so sexy that I almost relent. Instead I graze his asshole with a single slippery finger to distract myself and give him some motivation.

Finally, gasping between words, he says, "Please...fuck me... with your cock."

"Since you asked so nice." I don't hesitate to slide the strap-on gently into him an inch at a time, sighing at the sweetness of feeling his warm opening accept it. With his legs tied as they are, it takes only a palm on the inside of each thigh to hold them down and aside, exposing him completely. This doesn't keep him from trying to wrap them around me, the struggle making thrusting into him fully now all the more enjoyable.

It's a lovely sight watching my fake dick disappear into his ass over and over as I keep his thighs apart. When I have a steady pace going, I watch as instead of pushing his behind against me, he switches to furrowing his brow while making pained whimpers. His cock is straight in the air, dancing to the rhythm of my penetrating him and I can tell he's trying very hard not to come yet.

"Are you going to make a mess for me?" His eyes lock on mine. He nods, wrinkling his face in concentration. His desire to behave is greater than his need to climax. I grin at him as he watches me reach for his cock and stroke it. It's difficult to tell if he's glad for the stimulation or can't believe I'm being this mean to him. I feel him clench down on my rubber toy inside him. He makes animalistic noises as I continue fucking his ass and stroking his cock in the same tempo, unsure how he contains himself. I stop playing with his cock long enough to say, "Okay, be a good boy and come for me."

He looks at me gratefully as I use my aching palm to rub circles around the ridge of his glans just the way he likes. I plant my strap-on inside him so I can focus on rubbing his neglected cock. It isn't long before he shoots a pearly mess over his belly, giggling at the great relief after so much buildup.

His asshole relaxes around my dildo as he composes himself, his breathing going steady. As I lean down to begin untying him, I purposefully rest my belly in the sticky come that covers his furry belly and say, "You are such a good boy."

TIGHT-ROPE WALKER

Tilly Hunter

"It was your idea, remember," Jake said as we puffed up the hill with all the other Sunday afternoon ramblers.

"I know, but I didn't quite realize how walking in it would make me feel."

"Too late to change your mind now. Even if I was inclined to take it off, which I'm not, there's nowhere secluded to do it."

He was right. It had been my idea to climb the 1,335 feet of Wrekin, one of the most popular family strolls in England's West Midlands while wearing a *karada*, a rope body harness. And there was indeed nowhere secluded where Jake could take it off me. We'd come out of the trees half a mile back and now the terrain was just bare stones and scrubby grass.

Jake had practiced the various harness possibilities several times since getting into the more intricate *shibari* bondage. But never before had I strode out for miles uphill while wearing it under my clothes, and I'd had no idea of how it would feel. No idea of the tantalizing but unsatisfying friction against my clit, the rawness as it rubbed the tender membranes of my pussy and ass, the difficulty taking the deep inhalations I needed against the rope around my chest and belly. It was deep discomfort of the kind I liked best.

"Stop a sec," he said. I did so and he came up behind me just like any other amorous husband might do during a country walk with his beloved. "Maybe if I do this, it will help take your mind off it. Just until we get to the top, and then it's all plain sailing downhill and home." He grasped my wrists, pulled them behind me and linked the cuffs that were hidden between the sleeves of my fleece jacket and my thick woolen gloves.

I gasped and my body jerked involuntarily, pressing back into him. But my mind was rebelling. "You can't do that with all these people around. It's going to be bloody obvious. I might see someone I know, for god's sake."

"While I was walking behind you, I noticed you often clasp your hands behind your back on the steeper sections anyway. No one is going to see a thing." He had his arms around me now and I instinctively leaned my head back against his shoulder, baring the side of my neck for a kiss or a nip. But my neck was wrapped in a scarf, to hide my collar, and Jake neither kissed nor nipped. He just whispered in my ear, "So shut the fuck up and walk or I'll make you keep it on all day. And you can suck me off when we get home with no relief for yourself." He was joking. At least, I think he was joking. But sometimes he surprises me.

I walked. I grabbed one wrist in the other hand to make it look like I was indeed just clasping them behind my back to balance the forward-leaning posture as I struggled uphill. The rope ran from its central point, lying between my shoulder blades, over my shoulders to a knot at my chest. Its double length, knotted twice more, passed over my belly and pubic mound, snug between my legs and back up to its starting point.

So far so simple. But then Jake had done the beautiful diamond pattern he now knew so well. The rope ends wrapped under my armpits and through the two strands just above that knot at my chest. From there they parted again to pass over the tops of my breasts, thread through the loop at my shoulder blades and back to the front. All the way down my torso they threaded, hugging my breasts tight, wrapping my waist tight. Each pass pulled the downward strands between my legs a little more snugly into my pussy. I knew I had made those sections of rope wet.

I wasn't yet sure whether I regretted having the idea. It was now January, and it had already seemed a long and cold winter. The thing was, Jake and I had discovered the delights of outdoor sex and bondage the previous summer. Or rather, I'd finally revealed to him what my imagination got up to while we were cozy in bed, and he'd reacted with enthusiasm. He'd tied me to the trunks of trees, strung me up from branches, spread-eagled me on the earth with tent pegs, even hog-tied me in the shallows of a secluded beach where each incoming wave had made me gasp and splutter for breath. He had enough sense to do it while the tide was going out. But autumn had come, temperatures had dropped and we hadn't been out for our fun and games for months.

"Why don't you tie me into a harness I can hide under my clothes while we go out for a walk?" I'd said to him earlier that week, fed up with waiting for gray January skies to clear and the warmth of the sun to return. "You could even put on my collar and cuffs. If I wear a scarf and gloves, no one will see a thing. But it will make me horny as hell all the time we're walking. And then it will be there, ready, when we get home again."

Me and my big ideas. "Hmm, sounds like a plan," he'd said. "Forecast's dry for the weekend. We should do it on Sunday. We're going to my mother's for dinner Saturday, remember?"

I remembered. It felt like a very long evening of nodding in the right places and laughing and saying, "Oh yes, I know what you mean," rather than "Oh, just shut up so I can fantasize about rope."

We'd gotten up late and had a big cooked breakfast, as befits a lazy Sunday morning. Then, around noon, Jake said to me, "Pajamas off. Time for our walk." God, I'd thought that moment would never come. I was out of my PJs in seconds and standing, waiting, in the middle of the living room rug.

He put the collar around my neck first, as always. My collar. One-inch-thick leather that buckled into place. No lock, because I would never dream of attempting to remove it myself. But it did have four D-rings placed around it to account for all eventualities. He put similar leather cuffs on my wrists, then my ankles. These ones had simple karabiner-type clips to attach them to each other. If I was feeling brattish, I could escape them. Not easily, but it wasn't impossible. That's why Jake always used rope if he wanted me properly helpless.

Anyway, he moved on to the *karada* next. It had its usual effect on me, making my pussy pulse and my knees weak from the moment I felt the rope draped down the front of my body. As Jake pulled each wrap through the vertical strands, the vibrations went straight to my clit. I rocked my hips, smiling at the utterly delicious pressure there. He was careful not to tie it too tight and had used three-eighths-inch cotton to stop it from cutting into me. Once he was done, I put on my walking outfit, all sensible shower-proof fabrics, sturdy shoes with big grips and my winter woolens—hat, scarf, gloves. No panties though. And I pulled on a sporty crop top instead of trying to do up a bra strap over the ropes around my rib cage. As I moved around the house, up and down stairs and from room to room, I felt the harness hug my pussy snugly and imagined it doing so on our walk.

How wrong I was. Ambling around your house is nothing like actually taking a walk. A real, brisk walk over rough terrain.

I started off swinging my hips and grinning at the stimulation as the ropes ground from side to side over my clit. That didn't last long. Soon I was gasping at the sheer friction against tender places and the bite of restraint against parts of my torso that needed to rise and fall with my deep, hill-climbing breaths.

"How's it going?" Jake asked, winking, as I stopped for a rest for the first time.

"Fuck," I gasped. "It's rubbing in all the wrong places. My ass is so sore. As for my pussy, I wouldn't be surprised if I'm actually bleeding. And I can't breathe properly." I wanted to stick my hands down my pants and pull the ropes off my tender parts. But yet another family party, toddler in a rucksack carrier and older child moping behind, passed us. I hoped I was exaggerating about the bleeding. I like a little pain, but blood just makes me squeamish. I was pretty sure I was exaggerating.

I walked a lot more gingerly from then on, being as economical as possible with my strides and keeping my body upright and rigid. He was right though when he stopped me to link my wrist cuffs behind my back. It did take my mind off it. Suddenly, I welcomed the discomfort and the challenge of regulating my breathing.

I was in a world of my own as we headed toward the summit, being downright rude to those who said hello as they passed. Freed from the temptation to grab at the harness and shift the friction, I took it one step at a time, breathing hard. My clit throbbed against the pull and hitch of the rope. It made me wonder whether a tongue or finger would feel soothing there later, or like a further irritation of the tenderized spot.

I reached the viewpoint at the top and leaned sideways against it, trying now to make my hands-behind-my-back pose look natural. Jake was right behind me. He could have passed me and got there first, but I knew he preferred to watch my ass flexing as I moved up the slope. He stepped behind me and turned me to face the concrete pillar of the viewpoint, pressing his crotch into my crushed hands. Regardless of the passersby, he reached beneath my scarf and hooked a finger around the D-ring at the back of my collar, pulling my head into him so my back arched. I whimpered very quietly, hoping the breeze would carry the sound away. I was still trying to catch my breath and felt the collar's pressure on my windpipe all the more acutely.

Jake pressed against me and I felt his cock stiff against my fingers. "I want you so much," he murmured in my ear. "I can't wait to get you home and fuck you hard. I'm going to take my pleasure, then I'm going to make you come with my tongue while my knuckles stretch your cunt wide open." My stomach tingled in a way that had nothing to do with hunger. If he hadn't been crushing me against the pillar, I might have sunk to my knees right there. "You're going to spend the rest of the day tied up and I'm going to make you come over and over until you can't take any more." I loved it when Jake told me all the things he wanted to do to me. But I was in silent mode myself, that mindset where you don't need a gag because you simply can't form words anymore.

He pulled back and unclipped my wrists. "You're more likely to slip going downhill," he said, then in a louder voice, "Come on, let's get home and warmed up."

He took my hand, and we turned back the way we'd come. That's when I realized how the harness had shifted as I'd hunched forward uphill. It had gradually pulled longer over my rounded back and shoulders, shortening down the front. Of course, going downhill meant my balance switched the other way. The ropes dragged mercilessly, pulling my labia and the soft inner slit of my ass forward again. I gritted my teeth and carried on, longing to be tied to the bed in comfort. I was on the edge of what I thought I could bear.

We didn't stop until we got to the car. The relief of sitting still in the passenger seat was instant, but the flesh between my legs throbbed. I sat there afraid to move an inch, focusing on the few minutes it would take to get home.

Jake had other ideas. He turned down a quiet country lane. "What are you doing?" I gasped. "I need to get home. Now."

"I can't wait until we get home." He pulled into a lay-by and turned off the engine. "I need to be in you."

I started with a "But—" He got out of the car and shut his door on my protests.

Opening my side, he told me to get out and take my pants off. "I want you on all fours on the backseat, cunt at the door." I pulled my pants over my walking shoes and crawled into the back, stopping with my knees on the edge of the seat, ass in the doorway. At least he'd opened the door facing the hedgerow and not the road. He stood behind me and yanked the ropes apart between my legs, making my ass gape and exposing my pussy. The constriction at my waist tightened as he pulled. I felt the tip of his cock at my entrance as he struggled to guide it in while holding the harness aside. Finally the head slid inside and he rammed the rest of it home, his fingers trapped between his pelvis and my butt. He dragged his hands free and grabbed the ropes at the small of my back to pull me hard against him.

"Your ropes are squeezing my shaft really hard," he said. "I like it. I like being tied deep inside you. But I'm going to have to do something about them so I can fuck you before my balls implode. I'm going to cut the rope."

"No." It was the first thing I'd said for over an hour. I wasn't prepared to be freed yet. "You can't."

"Yes, I can. And I can punish you later for trying to tell me what to do." The games we play. I love them. My mind flashed with memories of spankings. I felt cold metal against the base of my spine and realized he was slicing through the rope with his pocketknife. The cotton weave ground harder against my clit as the blade worked against it and then it twanged loose. Jake began to pound into me urgently. The cut ends of the rope slipped out of place and my clit felt abandoned. I dropped to my elbows and braced myself against his solid thrusts. All too soon I felt Jake's cock grow and pulse inside me as he emptied his load with a loud groan.

He rested inside me for a moment. "Don't think I'm all done now," he said. "I'm still going to keep you tied up for the rest of the day at home. And I'm going to use the red ball gag to stop you telling me what to do again." The red gag was the largest one we owned. It made my jaw ache and the saliva drip from the corners of my mouth. It was the only one that really prevented speech with any real effectiveness.

"But now, I'm going to make you come. Hands behind your back please." Resting my forehead on the car seat's velour I shifted my arms behind me and Jake linked my cuffs. "Now turn over." He helped me squirm around and I wriggled my wrists until my hands were flat beneath the small of my back. My shoes smeared mud on Jake's shoulders. He took the two strands of loose rope and teased my clit for a moment, pulling them taut and jerking them from side to side. I lifted my hips and ground myself against them.

He tucked the strands out of the way, parted my labia and flicked the very tip of his tongue over my clit. Fuck. It was like a sharp note that made the usual sensation seem flat. That tiny lick shot straight into the depths of my pelvis. It felt as though the nerves of my clit were exposed directly to each minute ridge and fall of his taste buds.

He flicked at me again, and I disintegrated into a mess of desperate groans. A truckers' trailer café could have set up shop next to us in the lay-by and I couldn't have uttered a single word of protest as drivers leered through the car windows. Jake pushed two fingers inside me, quickly followed by a third. The sharp note of my pleasure notched up an octave as he set to the serious task of rasping the flat of his tongue up from the very base of my clit to its tip. His fingers slithered in his own come as he pushed his knuckles against my entrance with an exquisitely slow twist. I was there in seconds. At that peak, my second summit of the day, the view was all rainbows and pink mist.

"Oh fuck, I'm gonna come, I'm gonna come." I don't know what always compels me to confess this obvious fact, but I did it anyway and Jake moaned into my pussy as my body tightened and my eyes screwed shut. The orgasm carried on way past the moment I expected it to subside. It carried on so long I had to remind myself to breathe. It carried on so long that I opened my eyes again and watched the rainbows fizz against gray plastic the color of January clouds. "Fuck, stop," I finally groaned and Jake slowed, giving me a gentle last lick before stopping. He slipped his fingers out and lowered my limp legs to dangle out of the car door.

"That seemed intense." He walked his hands up the car's interior so he could reach my lips with his own. I couldn't answer. I could barely kiss back. "Let's get home. And get you comfortably tied to the bed." How does he always know what I'm thinking? But then came the surprise. "Next time we go for a walk, I'm going to put a butt plug into your lovely ass before I tie the *karada*. And you'll have to lose the crop top. I want you in nipple clamps."

AN APPRECIATION FOR BEAUTIFUL THINGS

Giselle Renarde

The antique mirror wore its age with pride—black splotches, veining and all. After Dell bought it, he removed the backing and popped off the gaudy gold frame. He didn't plan on hanging it.

Clearing the clutter from Genevieve's night table, Dell set the mirror down flat. *Perfect*—an ideal showcase for the gorgeous silver hairbrush that had come down through her family. That brush had started life paired with an equally ornate dressing table mirror. Splitting them up? That was his mother-in-law's bright idea. That's how Genevieve ended up with the lonely brush while her sister walked away with a hand mirror.

Not that it mattered anymore. Dell had found an alternate partner for Genevieve's brush, and their wabi-sabi union was beautiful in its own right.

He asked her to close her eyes as he guided her into the bedroom.

"Okay, now open them."

Genevieve looked around, like she was searching, searching,

searching...for something different. Dell saw in her face when she found it. She smiled rather more gently than he'd anticipated, and said, "You cleaned my night table."

"Yes, that, too." Dell pulled Genevieve to the bedside. "But look—I found a mirror to go with your brush. I cleaned them—don't worry, I was careful to preserve the patina—and set them out so you'd see them first thing every morning."

"Oh, neat." Her smile was fake. "Looks good. Everything you put together looks good. That's why I leave the decorating to you."

She obviously wasn't excited about the remarriage of vanity pieces, and that hurt Dell in a way he couldn't fully articulate.

"You don't like it."

"No, I do. I really do." She flopped on the bed and groaned. "Sorry, it's not you. Just one of those days."

He sat beside her, brushing pale orange wisps from her eyes. Despair didn't suit her pixie face, but he couldn't fathom what had upset her.

"Is there anything I can do?" he asked.

"No, just..." With a heaving breath, she sat up. "My mom thinks you're gay."

"I know. She's not exactly shy with the flagrant accusations." Dell stared into Genevieve's quixotic green eyes, but he didn't find what he was looking for. "What are you so worried about?"

She looked helplessly to the night table. "You're not...are you...?"

"You're asking if I'm *gay*?"

She smiled, and then laughed, and then rolled her eyes. "Sorry. I'm an idiot. It's my mom—she's poison."

"No, no—I get it." Dell wrapped his arms around his wife and kissed her hair. "Only a gay man can have an appreciation for beautiful things. How ridiculous is that? Aren't straight men supposed to have an appreciation for beautiful women?"

"You're right." She chuckled softly. "It doesn't make any sense."

"I'll never be your caveman," he said in all seriousness. "I love you. I desire you. I would give my life for you. But I'll never be a belching, beer-swilling brute. That's not who I am."

"Thank god." Her eyes darkened. "I mean, half your appeal is that you're...the way you are."

Dell cocked his head. "Gay-ish?"

"Yeah." Genevieve crept a little closer. When her fingers found his thigh, she dug her nails in hard, like she was hanging on for dear life. She wore a playful sneer when she said, "Ask any girl if she wants to fuck a gay guy, and you know what she'll say?"

"Yes?" Dell guessed.

"No." Genevieve found his hardness. "She'll say she wants to fuck *all* the gay guys."

Dell gasped as she rubbed his cock through his clothing. "Why?"

"I don't know. Maybe it's just a nice fantasy because we know it could never happen. It's a crush you can hold on to forever. It'll never go sour."

"You're just full of surprises," Dell said, pinning his wife to the mattress.

She gasped, eyes wide. "You, too."

"So tell me..." Dell writhed against her clothed body, rubbing his erection over her mound. "How many crushes do you have right now?"

"On gay guys, you mean?" She giggled, until he pressed his weight more firmly against her pelvis. "Oh, wow. Okay, maybe...six?"

Dell dropped his chest to hers, feeling the subtle rise and

swell of her breasts. He wasn't heavy, except in comparison to her. Trapped beneath him, she squirmed—not to escape, but to strike her sweet spot against his hardness. He knew her tricks, and he could tell when she'd found what she was looking for by the way her breath hitched.

"Six guys?" Dell's hot breath bounced off Genevieve's ear, kissing his lips. "Six gay men all oiled up and ready to fuck?"

"Yes."

His cock throbbed against her pussy. "What would they do to you?"

"I don't know." Genevieve swallowed hard as his hands found her ass. "I never really thought about the specifics."

He unzipped his pants and pulled out his erection. He couldn't wait any longer. Just listening to her talk like that, so dirty, about all those guys...

"If they were here in this room, right now, what would they do?"

"Fuck me," Genevieve moaned.

"They'd fuck you? All six of them?"

"No, *you*!" She yanked up her skirt. "I want *you* to fuck me, Dell."

He held her shoulders against the bed and raised his hips. "Pull your panties down if you want to get fucked so bad."

"What, you don't believe me?"

"I'll believe it when I see it, sister." His cockhead whacked her belly. "You don't seem to be in any hurry to get those panties off."

Genevieve peeled their clothes away wildly, throwing everything everywhere. Dell wasn't even sure how he got out of his pants, but the fine fabric ended up on the floor, just like everything else.

"There," she cried. "Happy now?"

"Not yet." Dell held her down as he guided his cock to her cunt. She groaned when his throbbing tip swelled in the wet heat between her thighs. "That's more like it."

Genevieve whimpered as he savored the warm hug of her pussy. When she tightened up, god, she was a vise around his shaft. Her cunt sucked his dick like a practiced mouth. There was no containing Little Miss Genevieve. Dell could hold her body down, but her pussy was its own universe, exerting every possible pressure. It was too good, too much.

"Fuck, I can't." He pulled out, crawling off the bed.

"What's wrong?"

"I'm about to come."

"Already?"

"I just need a little..." Dell's gaze fell across the night table. "Brush."

Genevieve panted as she watched him. "You need a little brush?"

Something rugged and rough burbled up inside Dell, making his cock throb. His dick was drenched in pussy juice. He could smell it on him like a wet musk.

Yanking Genevieve's calves, he drew her to the edge of the mattress. She screamed when he flipped her little body upside down, letting her legs dangle off the side of the bed.

"What are you doing, Dell?"

"I'm spanking you, Little Miss."

He couldn't quite tell if that was a giggle or a fearful squeal.

"Oh god," she whispered. "Okay."

Dell picked up the gorgeous silver brush. "I'm spanking you with *this*."

"Oh." Her fingers clenched around the duvet. Dell could feel a squeal rising in her throat as he brought the brush down—but not too hard, not to start.

Genevieve pulled more of the duvet under her breast, forming herself a feathery nest. "More?"

"Yes." Dell brought the wide paddle of the brush down on her ass. Harder, this time. Hard enough to make her scream. She sounded almost surprised, like she hadn't seen it coming.

"Too much?"

"No," Genevieve whimpered. "No, it's good. Keep going."

His cock surged, whacking her thigh as he traced the paddle around her virgin cheek. He was just about to spank her when his hand took control of the scene. Flipping the brush, he carved her flesh with the cruel horsehair bristles.

"Ouch." Genevieve whacked the brush away with one hand. "That really hurts."

"Does it?" He flipped the brush over, and slammed it down on her fresh cheek.

She shrieked, obviously unprepared for the force of that spanking. "Ow!"

"More?"

"Yes," she whimpered.

He paddled her again, more than once. After three passes at the same spot, she started swatting at the brush.

"No!" Dell said. "Bad girl. Keep your hands to yourself."

He smacked the other cheek to give the pinkish one a bit of a break, but Genevieve kept swatting. "I can't help it. My hands have a mind of their own."

"Well, control them." Dell grabbed her wrist and held it at the small of her back.

"I can't!"

When he brought the silver brush down, he didn't see her other hand swooping in to block it. Until he'd slammed the business end against her ass, he didn't even realize her fingers had gotten in the way.

"Dell!" Genevieve's body tensed, visibly, as she brought her fingers to her mouth. "Shit, that hurts."

"Sorry. Are you okay?" He dropped the brush and walked naked around the bed. "Here, let me kiss it better."

She held out her finger and pressed it against his lips. "Hurts like hell."

He kissed it better, then kissed her lips. "You obviously can't be trusted to keep your body in check."

"What's that supposed to mean?"

Dell untied the thick ribbon that held the bedroom curtains open. "It means that you need a little help."

The black satin looked like a million bucks against Genevieve's pinkish skin. He wrapped it around her wrists, securing her hands above her head. *There.* Now she couldn't swat at the brush while he whacked her. She looked good facedown on the white duvet with a long black ribbon tied around her wrists.

"That's better," he said, rubbing his erection across her hands. He leaned over and kissed her hair while her fingers struggled to grasp his dick. "Now back to work."

"Is it work, making love to me?"

Genevieve's question struck Dell as passive-aggressive and displaced, so he ignored it. He wasn't going to engage. Picking up the brush, he stood between her slightly opened legs. His cock pointed the way like a dowsing rod, but he wouldn't surrender to her pussy. Not just yet.

"Are you ready?" he asked.

"For what?"

He brought the paddle down on her firm ass. "For that."

Genevieve whimpered as he spanked her. His paddling fell in measured beats against her cheeks—one, then the other—and he sort of wished she had more meat on her bones. Her body was neat and spare. Her flesh didn't ripple when struck. Dell wouldn't mind spanking a Jell-O body and watching the fat flail. But he wouldn't tell Genevieve a thing like that.

"It hurts," she whined, straining to look at him. Her eyes widened. "Let me suck your cock."

Dell struggled against his dick's desire. He spanked her hard. "Not yet."

"Please?"

A meek shudder ran down his spine as he gripped the brush tighter. "Soon."

He whacked her ass, watching her hands struggle against the satin ribbon. He'd tied it well. She couldn't escape, no matter how hard she tried. She cursed him and cried as he paddled her.

When he heard tears in her voice, he said, "I can stop."

She whimpered, but didn't say a word.

Turning the brush around, Dell gripped the big silver paddle. Slowly, he pushed the bulbous handle into her pussy. "How's that?"

She groaned, like she couldn't bear the intensity. "Ohhh..."

He fucked her with the brush—not too slow, not too fast—and, god, his cock was jealous. "Tell me if I should quit spanking you."

"Ohhh..."

"You need to tell me, or I'll keep doing it. Your little hands can't stop me. They're all tied up in pretty black ribbon."

Genevieve moaned as Dell turned the handle in her wet pussy. Her feet didn't touch the floor. Strung across the mattress like that, she was pretty much immobilized. Totally in his control.

"You don't want me to stop, do you?" Dell pulled the handle from her cunt, making her whimper. "You want me to paint your ass pink. You want me to carve all these pretty little flowers into your flesh and make you cry."

"Yes," she whispered.

"What's that?" He traced the wet handle around her pussy lips, nudging her clit. "I didn't hear you."

She swallowed hard. "Yes."

"Yes, please?"

Genevieve squirmed against the bed. Her fingers fluttered. "Yes. Please."

Dell's palm slipped on the brush handle. It was slick with pussy juice. The paddle's rosebud pattern carved its way down the fat base, and he wondered if his hand would end up tattooed with flowers. Genevieve's ass certainly would be.

He smacked her hard. After all her shy pleading, Dell knew what she wanted. Every time the paddle met her ass, a resounding crack danced around the room. That sound turned him on almost as much as Genevieve's unhindered screams.

"Does it hurt?" he asked, taunting her.

"Yes!" she shrieked even before he'd brought the brush down on her raw flesh. She shrieked even louder when the silver paddle kissed her ass. "Fuck! Oh god, it hurts."

Dell's cock throbbed wickedly as he punished her. His tip glowed almost as deep a red as Genevieve's rosy cheeks. The only difference? His dick wasn't painted with roses.

"Look at me, Little Miss."

She turned her head, though it was obviously difficult with her arms tied up. Tears streaked her face, but her lips wore a grin. She whispered, "Don't stop."

Her raw ass radiated such violent heat that he could feel it against his thigh. He turned the brush around, relishing her whimpers as he slowly fucked her with the handle. His dick throbbed indecisively—pussy or mouth? God, her asshole puckered, too, begging for a little something. How was he supposed to decide?

"I think you've had enough," he told her, pulling the handle from her cunt.

She whined, but Dell stood firm. He could give pain like a gift, but he had no desire to harm her. Anything more would tip the balance toward injury.

"Anyway," he said, "I thought a certain someone wanted to suck a certain something."

He walked around the bed, greeted by the smile on Genevieve's lips. Grabbing her arms, he yanked her tiny body forward until her laced-up wrists hung down the side of the mattress. She chased his bulging cockhead with her tongue as it slapped her face, spilling precome across her cheek. God, she looked great like that—anxious, aroused, yet somehow alleviated.

She took his cock between her lips, and her mouth was so wet and warm he struggled to stay upright. He could have filled her throat right away, but he held out, digging his fingers into her hair. She sucked gently, then harder, drawing his dick in deep. His hips moved of their own volition. He fucked her face. God, she was beautiful. Those sweet little pixie lips sucked the life out of him.

He didn't want to come yet, but he couldn't hold out. When his climax took hold, he felt it in his balls. He felt it in his knees. His whole body pulsed with orgasm as he flowed into her.

"Dell?" Genevieve shook her head, dropping his spent cock from her lips. Droplets of come spilled down her bound arms. "Dell, can I ask you a question?"

"Huh?" His ears hummed so loudly he could barely hear. Dizzied by orgasm, he swerved onto the bed. "What's up?"

"You would tell me, right?" She looked up at him beseechingly, flashing her barely there lashes.

"Tell you what?"

"You know." She looked away, down at the carpet. "If you were gay."

Dell's brain buzzed. Genevieve asked that question pretty

much every time she got off the phone with her mother. She would never stop asking. When people perceived you as gay, it was a lot like them thinking you were in denial—you couldn't disprove their opinions without protesting too much.

MIND FUCK

Kissa Starling

Quinton stands at the foot of the bed, gazing. She wears nothing, as instructed. Plumped-up pillows prop her arms on each side. More padding lifts her calves and feet, thighs parted, displaying her luscious center. Her chestnut hair cascades behind her head, curling on the ends close to her shoulder.

He steps over to her, opening his fingers wide above her wrists. Two small pieces of packing tape and a ball gag lie in his hand. He touches his warm lips to hers, mimicking the insertion of the gag. Cool air passes where their lips part. The gag sits beneath her chin as a reminder.

"I hereby secure you, Cari; my fingers weave bindings across your forearm." He bends to kiss the inside of her wrist; his tongue trails to the crook in her elbow. "Your wrists and arms are immobile. The tape secures you to the bed." His fingers pause at her breasts. The tiny amount of adhesive bonds to her delicate skin.

"Your pink rosy nipples will be scarlet red when I finish

with them." His palms push her large breasts together until the nipples touch. He covers them with his mouth, raking down with his front teeth over the peaks. She gasps beneath him. Her shoulders press into the sheets and her pelvis tilts. Her breathing quickens. His tongue lathers thin marks left behind. Cari shakes her chest and whimpers when the bindings limit her reach.

He rises, pinching her right nipple with his nail and setting a piece of twine across her breasts. It is attached to nothing. "Don't let that fall, my sweet," he whispers.

His palm encases one nipple, creating a suction pocket. The other hand rubs rapidly, heating the flesh beneath. Fingers come together, grasping the hardened nipple. "I circle this perfect piece of flesh with twine that only you and I can see." One nail touches the base of the valley, circling her breast. Faster and faster, circling until the peak is reached and then two nails dig into the flesh. He lifts the twine and tugs. Cari closes her eyes, moaning. He turns on the monitor by the bed. "My finger hooks and yanks the taut twine connection." One shrill scream fills the room.

A few minutes later silence replaces the scream. "I crisscross your fleshy belly using my special braided rope and fishhook around your thighs. Settle into your position, my sweet. There's no escaping now." Quinton sucks the skin surrounding her belly button and his tongue delves in. He lays the rope in a circle to surround her button. Cari squirms, her bottom wiggling. His ministrations continue along the inside of her right thigh. She attempts to raise herself closer to his mouth, but is stopped short. He laughs at her bungled endeavor. "You do remember the rope."

Her fingers bend. She motions for him to come closer. "No, no, my pretty. I didn't eat when I got home. I hope you left dinner in the microwave as I noted on my list." Cari nods yes.

He turns the light off. A nightlight leaves a soft glow by the bed. Her eyebrows draw together, her pupils grow wide and her lower lip pokes out.

"Now, dear. You know I need sustenance if I'm to please myself this evening." She sobs as he closes the door. Quinton finds roast and mashed potatoes in the microwave. He flips on the companion monitor to listen. Other than heavy breathing he hears nothing.

He punches the button down, mic on. "The rope pushes into your delicate skin. Fraying ends prick like needles, leaving irritable red dots behind. Your nipples harden and your full breasts strain against the twine I've bound around them. It cuts into the bumpy areolas, creating staple-like marks. These signs indicate ownership. You are mine, my sweetest Cari. Never forget that."

The monitor goes back into the charger while he finishes dinner. He longs to see her reaction to his words, but there's plenty of time for that later. Unbeknownst to his beloved, a hidden camera tapes her every movement. They'll watch it together, cuddled, once he unbinds her.

Quinton checks the clock above the range; ten thirty. It's been fifteen minutes. Anticipation builds, but he won't leave her much longer. Waiting is the hardest part for him. She plays the part so well. He washes his hands and then undresses, folding each piece and laying it over the chair, listening in case she needs him. It's time. His hand turns the knob of the bedroom door. He no longer needs the monitor to hear her sniveling cries of desperation.

"Oh, Cari. I'm here." His words are long and drawn out. He slams the door behind him and pounces onto the bed. "I plan to devour you." Quinton lifts his leg to straddle Cari's middle. "I'm removing your gag. Stretch your mouth and lick your lips." He lifts a glass of water to her lips and she drinks while he throws the real gag to the carpet. "Good girl." Her lips expand into a smile. She rubs her head against his thigh. A tongue pokes out, lifting toward him. She isn't speaking yet, but he knows what she wants. He strokes his cock in front of her mouth. Saliva forms around the corners of her mouth. She licks repeatedly.

Please? Her mouth forms the word, but no voice accompanies it.

"Of course, my dear." Quinton rubs the head on her lip and across her cheek. She inhales, eyes closed. "Excites you, doesn't it?"

"Rose." The word is spoken so softly he almost misses it; her timing surprises him. Five more minutes is her limit in this position. He demanded new safewords when they found out about the degenerate muscle disease. Quinton wants to stop, but that isn't what she needs. He will give her a few minutes and then change things around. No embarrassment for either of them.

Cari holds her tongue out, flat. He loves how she continues the scene without missing a beat. His cock lies on top of her tongue. She draws it into her mouth, matching his long thrusts in and out.

Quinton leans back to unwind the rope from her thighs. No words are needed. He holds the real rope in his hand, sliding it along her innermost areas and then throwing it to the side. Cari stretches her legs, straight and taut above the pillows. Her torso relaxes onto the mattress. He props himself back on his hands, lifting his cock to fuck her slick mouth. Faster thrusts, in and out. At the last minute, he leans forward, holding to the headboard, fucking her warm, wet tunnel.

The noise of his cock entering her excites him. Cari extends her neck toward the wall. He reaches down and cups the back of her neck, forcing his cock deeper down her throat. Intense pleasure explodes. Both palms on the wall above the headboard. His knees stiffen, his cock withdraws and come spurts all over Cari's face. She closes her eyes, but flicks her tongue back and forth, licking all that she can.

"Very good, my come slut." Quinton slips his hand beneath the twine binding her nipples and jerks. She tenses. A scream erupts from deep inside her throat. Gurgling continues for a full minute. He removes the nonexistent rope from her belly and the arm bindings that aren't really there while she watches, desire filling her pupils.

Quinton massages her arms and hands. He kisses her elbows, knees and hips, all of the joint areas that wreak havoc on her supple body. "The feeling should be coming back now." His words cue her. Cari sits up. "Not so fast." He washes her face, using a cloth from the bedside table. "New position. I'll bind your wrists and your ankles together. On your stomach." She flips over without speaking. Her bottom lifts up. Cari looks behind at him. Her gaze follows his movements. He sees the need to please there.

"I'm using strips of leather for your ankles." He pulls a leather shoelace tight between his thumbs. The leather lifts the skin a bit as he runs it from ankle to ass. "Put your arms in front of you. For these I'll use my favorite leopard scarf." He mimics the tying of the knots on her wrists where she can see. She laughs as he ties the real scarf into a bow and wraps it around her neck so that she can feel the texture of the fabric. "Lower your chest, my love."

His favorite position by far. Quinton pats the outside of her voluptuous bottom, squeezing to get a good feel. He reaches between her legs and pinches her clit. Her legs spread at the knees, but her ankles stay crossed. She has worked so hard the past few months. Her body must reminisce about past sessions for the mind play to work. Juices run from the center of her pussy. He shoves three fingers in, pumping furiously. She bucks and slams herself down, again and again. Her hips bump side to side. He trails the end of the rope along the small of her back.

"Come for me, my sweet." Her back curves up, a cat pose she's learned in yoga. He slaps her pussy, his middle finger pushing into her clit each time. "Let me hear your pleasure." He enunciates each word. Cari howls, head tucked under. As the orgasm travels, her shoulders rise and her head leans to touch her back. Shudders begin at her toes and voyage the length of her spine. Finally, total collapse.

Quinton's cock stirs. This woman electrifies him like no other. He removes his fingers and sucks her juices from his fingers. "So good, my girl." Cari shifts. He contemplates ending it for the night, but she lifts her ass to the tip of his cock. Semi-hard becomes fully hard. He needs her touch, her lust and, most importantly, her love.

His cock plunges inside her sloppy wet pussy. In and out, slowly at first and then faster. They work into a rhythm, their bodies move together, fucking as one. Quinton leans forward, plucking the knot on the imaginary silk scarf to release her wrist binding. "Use your fingers, Cari."

She vibrates her fingers back and forth across her mound, up to her tits and back to her clit. When she grabs both nipples and presses down with her thumbs, he bites the back of her neck, tugging the scarf with his teeth. A second's pause leads to furious fucking. Her whimpers turn into a full-throated scream. Quinton yells out and comes simultaneously. He kisses the small of her back, massages her shoulders and removes the leather ankle binds that aren't really there. He holds her calf and bends each leg, massaging before he gently lays each back on the sheet.

"Turn over, my love." Cari rolls onto her back, pulling her

knees up to her belly. Quinton stacks pillows against the head-board and sits up, guiding her toward his side. He lifts the top sheet and covers her always cold feet. Her head rests on his chest. It takes several minutes for her breathing to return to normal. He waits.

"Thank you, Sir." Their lips meet. His tongue enters her mouth and laps around her tongue, holding it still and then creating a tunnel to suck it intermediately. He kisses the tip of her tongue and her lips.

"I didn't last as long this time." Her expression changes in that instant.

"No, you didn't." His fingers rift through her damp hair.

"I love you." She rubs circles in his chest hair and kisses him on the shoulder.

"I know you do." He forces himself to stay quiet. She needs this time to sift through her feelings. His heart wants to pull her close and reassure her over and over that she will always be his, but his mind demands he give her time to process. This transi-tion is new territory for both of them.

"This works for us, for now, right?" A direct question has to be answered.

"It works for me, my dear. The way I bind you isn't so impor-tant as the way you react to it. How did it make you feel?" She hesitates. "The truth, Cari."

"The truth is I long for the ropes, the leather and the scarves you used to bind me with, but my body is assimilating. I feel the materials when the words come from your lips. It will only get better. Next time I'll open my mind even more. The bits of rope and material facilitate my sub zone."

"That is what the doctor suggested." He inches his body closer to hers, careful not to touch any joints.

She cuddles closer.

"I have one more surprise." He watches to gauge her reaction. Fear clouds her eyes.

His chest tightens. "No, dear. No more play tonight. How about a home movie?"

She laughs. A mischievous grin appears. There's his dear, his wife and, for as long as he can hold on to her, his life. He presses the button on the remote and Cari watches, wide-eyed, as her sexy, nude form fills the screen.

WEARING PURPLE

Elizabeth Coldwell

Standing with his back to the whipping post, naked but for a length of ribbon tied in a neat bow around his semierect penis and his wrists tethered behind him with the bright purple pashmina, he couldn't help but reflect that his wife certainly knew how to bear a grudge.

She must have been planning her revenge from the moment he pressed the hastily bought, even more hastily wrapped present into her hands on his return from his business trip to Belgium. For Ramona, Belgium meant one thing, and that was chocolate. Her only weakness, a box of it was never far from her plump, creamy fingers, ready for her to dip into. While she often grumbled about the extra pounds that had gathered on her hips and thighs as the years passed, he loved the look and feel of her abundant flesh, the weight of her body on his as they fucked.

When he told her he'd bring her back something she'd love, she'd dropped heavy hints about a master chocolatier she'd seen interviewed in one of the Sunday supplements. His exquisite handmade pralines, it was claimed, were those by which all others would be measured and found wanting. Nothing less would do for her, so how he ever thought she'd be satisfied with a pashmina instead, he still didn't know. His excuses that his business meeting had overrun and he hadn't had time to hunt for the chocolate shop had been greeted with cold-faced silence.

"I'll make it up to you, darling," he'd promised.

"Oh, I know you will," had been her reply. She'd all but thrown the length of fine cashmere material at him. "I mean, purple, of all colors. In all the years we've been married, when have you ever seen me wearing purple?"

In his haste, and in the subdued light of the railway station concession where he'd made his ill-advised purchase, he thought he'd chosen a wrap that matched the cornflower blue of Ramona's eyes. Lying discarded on the bed, its true shade became all too obvious, mocking his poor judgment. Another mistake, another demerit to add to the list his mistress carried in her head. Retribution would come, it always did. He just never knew when, or where, or even how. And that made it worse—and better, on so many levels.

Tonight began like any other party night. His outfit for the evening lay on the bed when he emerged from the bathroom showered, shaved and powdered. Snug-fitting leatherette shorts, socks and heavy black boots. Nothing else. His collar would be fitted around his neck in the moments before leaving the house, further emphasizing his status as lowly slave and Mistress Ramona's chattel.

His mistress waited for him downstairs, the taxi already ordered and on its way. As always, she looked magnificent: dressed from head to foot in shiny black rubber, a blue-and-black waist-cincher nipping her in around the middle and making a perfect hourglass of her curves. So worthy of his respect, his adoration, it was all he could do not to fall to his knees and worship her. That, he knew, would come later, with an audience present to witness his groveling show of obeisance. Keyed up and already almost unbearably horny, he didn't notice what she slipped into her latex shoulder bag in the moments before they left the house. If he'd been more observant, he might have had some inkling of how this evening would progress, and the humiliating position in which she intended to place him. Not that he'd have been able to prevent any of it. The only way he could have done that was by bringing her back the chocolate she craved.

When they'd walked into Club Strict, they'd been greeted by an effusive Sir Nigel, the club's regular host for the last five years and one of their oldest friends on the scene. This, however, was no ordinary night—Sir Nigel was holding his birthday party, for invited guests alone, and for one night only, just about anything went. There were none of the usual restrictions on public nudity or sexual interaction in the club environment. Still, the night was young, and as he'd made his way to the bar to order Mistress Ramona a gin and tonic, he'd seen little in the way of play. A bare-breasted blonde crawled on a leash in the wake of her stocky black master, and a balding, bespectacled slave he recognized as one of Sir Nigel's regular bridge foursome lapped at the feet of a redheaded mistress who chatted away to a friend, totally oblivious to the sub's presence. He wondered what the man's bridge partner would say if she saw him now, semi-clad and subservient, or whether she already knew he, like everyone else here, had a secret side he kept separate from his daily, vanilla life.

They'd been there more than an hour before any serious action began. In that time, he'd refreshed his mistress's glass once, and followed her obediently around the club, eyes downcast, as she'd sought out acquaintances and caught up on all the gossip. It was just like every other night at Club Strict, and he'd relaxed fully into his role, as he always did.

"Ladies and gentlemen, goddesses and worms, might I have your attention?" Sir Nigel's voice boomed out above the low, throbbing bass of the sound system. "Thank you for coming to my party and making my transition into my sixth decade such a delightfully depraved one. I've arranged a couple of special performances for you all tonight, and I'd like to present the first of those now. My very good friend Mistress Ramona is about to give a bondage demonstration, with the aid of her pathetic excuse for a submissive, Slave Graham…"

At the mention of his name, he'd stiffened to attention. His mistress had mentioned nothing about any such demonstration when they'd left the house tonight. Even before he could begin to wonder what she might have planned for him, she marched him over to one of the pieces of equipment set up in the club's central playroom—a sturdy, black-painted post, designed to allow a slave to be tethered to it for a whipping. A small crowd, the lithe, silver-haired figure of Sir Nigel prominent among them, began to gather round as his mistress ordered him to stand with his back to the whipping post, and to clasp his hands together behind himself, so that he effectively embraced the wooden structure.

"I know that many of you are constantly searching for new ways to restrain your submissive," Mistress Ramona was saying, as the audience hung on her every word, "and new methods of reinforcing your discipline. And it is very important that they know just how low it's possible for them to sink in your estimation, and how hard they must work to regain even a shred of respect."

His stomach churned with nauseous anticipation, the hairs on his arms and legs prickled to attention. The rebuke in her choice of words might not have been obvious to those watching, but he knew he was about to pay for his misdemeanors.

"Now," his mistress continued, "it's always nice to have good quality equipment to play with, like padded leather cuffs, silk bondage rope or even proper, police-issue handcuffs—eh, Mike?"

The man she'd addressed her comment to, a detective in the local force, chuckled gruffly and fingered the shiny silver cuffs that dangled from his belt.

"But what if you don't have your toy box with you, or you're experimenting with a little tie and tease? What might you use then?"

"Stockings," someone at the back of the crowd piped up, even though Ramona didn't appear to have been soliciting a response.

She shook her head. With her back to him, he couldn't see her expression, but he suspected she wore the patient smile that indicated a foolish answer had been given. "Many people think that, but cheap nylon stockings can be dangerous. When you pull on them, they keep tightening, and you never want to put your slave in something that can cut into their flesh. But there are plenty of things you can use instead. A necktie, a silk scarf, the sash of a dressing gown. We can all find something that's been shoved into a drawer, forgotten and unwanted. Something—" she paused, letting her previous words sink in "—like this."

Turning side on, she pulled an item from her shoulder bag with a theatrical flourish. Even in the dim light of the club, he recognized the all-too-familiar length of fine purple material.

"Now, I'm sure some of you remember the days when pashminas used to be fashionable..." His mistress shot him a look that dripped icy contempt; he felt as if his balls were trying to crawl up inside his body. "But now, they're really no good for anything apart from binding in place a worthless specimen such as the one I have here."

As she spoke, she moved behind the post. He felt the brush of soft cashmere against the skin of his forearms.

"If any of you would like to come round to this side, you'll get a better view of the knot, but I'm using a simple French bowline, so there'll be no risk of cutting off this wretch's circulation."

It was amazing, he thought, how she could express concern for his welfare in a tone suggesting that, given the choice, she'd cut off much more than that. Then the pashmina was being wrapped around his wrists and the thickness of the post—once, and then again, before his mistress tied the fabric in the knot she'd described. It placed no pressure against his flesh, but when he gave an experimental tug, he realized she'd bound him securely enough that he couldn't get free until she decreed it. An electric jolt shot through him, the thrill he always felt when his mistress placed him in bondage. Innately subservient to her will, he couldn't help but react when she enforced her domination over him, especially with more than a dozen pairs of eyes watching their scene unfold.

"So," his mistress said, "now that you have your slave in bondage, you have the opportunity to give them pleasure or pain. Or maybe just a spot of well-deserved humiliation."

Her hands clutched the elastic waistband of his shorts and tugged them down in one smooth movement. She let them settle around his knees, restraining him further. His cheeks burned with the shame of being stripped before an audience, even as his cock began to rise. He and Ramona had discussed a scenario like this so many times, but until tonight the circumstances had never been right for her to humiliate him so publicly.

And still she hadn't finished. Withdrawing something else from her bag, she bent to take hold of his cock. "Now, I know many of you mistresses favor the cock cage, and I'm sure more than one pathetic article has his manhood under lock and key tonight. But I find it's far more amusing to show up my slave for the sissy he is."

With that, she wrapped what he quickly realized was a piece of purple ribbon around his shaft, tying it in a big, floppy bow. A woman in the crowd tittered at the sight; her reaction should have made his cock wilt, but instead it surged up even harder.

"And that concludes my demonstration for the evening," his mistress said, receiving a rapturous round of applause. She made a brief curtsey of acknowledgment, then the spectators began to drift away, some to the bar, others to the dance floor, muttering among themselves about what they'd just witnessed.

"So, slave..." The words were a spiteful caress in his ear. He smelled the intoxicating scents of latex and her favorite spicy perfume, a mixture that would become even more potent when mingled with the aroma of her plump, rubber-encased sex. He itched to be on his knees, face buried in her crotch, breathing in that scent. "I trust I can leave you on your own for a little while, to allow you to contemplate the wisdom of buying your mistress such an unsuitable gift?"

"Yes, Mistress." The last thing he wanted was to be left alone. He needed to feel Ramona's fingers around his aching, beribboned dick, teasing a climax from him. But Sir Nigel was beckoning to her, telling her he had someone he'd like her to meet. And with that she was gone, leaving him to stew in his helplessness and frustration.

That had been, at his best guess, forty minutes ago, though it was impossible to gain any real sense of how quickly time passed in an environment with no clocks visible. All around him, the sights and sounds of a club night in full swing contrived to torment him. Somewhere behind him, he could hear the rhythmic thudding of some implement landing repeatedly on bare flesh—a paddle, he suspected—and the low, anguished moans of the girl being disciplined. Being unable to see the scene as it unfolded sent a shudder of longing through him, as his cock rose once more in response to the images flooding his mind: the rosy bloom on the girl's backside; the steadily falling arm of whoever was chastising her; the glistening juices on her pussy lips, as her body reacted on a purely physical level, turning pleasure into pain. Unable to turn in the direction of the noises, he stared straight ahead, hoping another couple might start to act out their own punishment ritual within his limited line of sight.

Despite the vulnerability of his position, he couldn't help but admire the ingenious way his mistress had used her hated gift against him. She'd taken care with his binding, and he felt no real discomfort apart from the slight ache in his back and shoulders that came from remaining in the same position for an extended length of time. She had treated him with loving cruelty, which was all he ever asked of her, but now he needed more.

Behind him, the girl's moans had taken on a sweeter quality, and he swore he could hear the squelching sounds of fingers being thrust in and out of her pussy. She had taken her punishment, and now came her reward. He groaned. If his mistress had intentionally sought to drive him into a vortex of frustration by binding him in place, she could not have chosen a more perfect spot. He couldn't escape from the aural evidence of someone else receiving the stimulation he craved so desperately.

As the moans peaked, fast and frantic, then died away to soft, satisfied whimpers, he silently begged for someone to offer him the same treatment. His cock stood up tight to his belly button, precome shining at its tip, revealing the full extent of his need. He didn't care who chose to use him—male or female, dominant or submissive. If only some master would order her slave to her knees, to take him in her mouth and suck him till his seed geysered down her soft, gulping throat. Or if the domina in the elbow-length red gloves he'd seen clapping politely at the end of his mistress's demonstration would wrap her leather-clad fingers around him, working them swiftly up and down his length. He could almost see the stains his white cream would leave on the supple red hide. For a moment, he even entertained the thought of someone taking a punishment implement to him, trailing the thongs of a soft suede flogger over his dick and balls, or rapping his swollen cockhead with a riding crop. The pain would be all the more delicious for being administered by someone he might not even know, someone who'd seen his helplessly restrained state and decided to take full advantage of it.

He writhed against the post, tugging at his bonds even though he knew he had no hope of getting free. If his mistress had chosen to tether him facing the post, he could have rubbed himself against the hard wood, creating just enough in the way of friction with his limited range of movement to bring himself off. Oh, he'd have paid for that afterward, he knew, but what was one more demerit on top of those he'd already earned?

Then, just as he'd slumped back into a resigned, defeated posture, shoulders sagging and cock beginning to deflate, he heard a familiar voice purr in his ear, "Purple may not suit me, but it certainly looks good on you. So, slave, have we learned our lesson?"

"Y-yes, Mistress," he stammered, instantly hard again despite the thought that she might not have finished tormenting him. Perhaps she'd only come to check on him before going back to her dominatrix friends, so they could all laugh at his frustrating predicament over more drinks.

"And will we be giving anything other than the finest quality chocolate as a present in future?"

"N-no, Mistress."

With that, she began to untie the ribbon that adorned his cock. Just the feeling of her long, cool fingers against his over-heated shaft was enough to have the come spurting from him to puddle at his feet.

"And you'll have to lick that up, won't you?"

"Yes, Mistress." His heart beat fast as she loosened the knot that held him in place, his body recovering from the force of his unexpected orgasm. Without pulling up his shorts, he dropped to his hands and knees, hearing the click and complaint of joints held immobile for so long. Under his mistress's watchful gaze, he obediently lapped up every creamy drop.

She ordered him to his feet once more and told him to make himself look respectable.

"Come on," she said, as he tucked his wilting cock back into his shorts, "let's go home. I'm sure Sir Nigel can carry on the party without us, and I have my own needs to attend to."

"So, I take it you'll be getting rid of the pashmina now, Mistress?" he said, as she stuffed it back into her shoulder bag, already thinking ahead to the moment when she would peel off the catsuit and order him to worship her body with his tongue. "After all, I'd venture to suggest it's served its purpose."

She shook her head. "The couple Sir Nigel introduced me to run a monthly fetish market, and they're always looking for people to run workshops and demonstrations. They'd like me—us—to attend the next event, and talk about how to enjoy bondage on a budget. Said using the pashmina was a really inspired touch. Oh, I won't be able to go quite as far as I did tonight—sadly, they won't allow me to expose that sissy cock of yours." She gave his bulge an affectionate squeeze through his shorts, smiling as he groaned with reawakening arousal. "But don't worry, my love, there are still plenty of other ways I can humiliate you with your clothes on."

His mind racing as he tried to imagine all the delightfully shameful things she could—and would—do to him the next time she had him bound with the pashmina, he followed her out to the cloakroom.

DUAL MASTERY

Rachel Kramer Bussel

Some people I've met in the kinky world think that owning a sex slave is easy. They consider the mere idea equivalent to a nonstop orgy, 24/7. I hate to bust their bubble—or yours—but while I love being a master to two women, I work hard to keep them happy, and in turn, I am amply rewarded. I wouldn't trade my life for a conventional one for millions of dollars, but a good master has to give as good as he gets—at least, that's my philosophy.

I'm not the kind of master who thinks my job is to be the sole provider for a household of three; in fact, I admire that both women are savvy go-getters in their careers. I love overhearing my wife Tanya negotiating prices for her jewelry supplies or seeing Wendy work a room for an event she's organized, knowing that for me and me alone (unless I've given permission otherwise) do they bow down, get on their knees, become women utterly unrecognizable from the powerhouse professionals they are in their respective business worlds, where they are revered and even feared by some. Where would the magic be in conquering a woman who already appears to be conquered by the world? I'll pass on that.

With three incomes, we are more than comfortable, which allows for plenty of time off, sometimes spent in our home dungeon, sometimes simply curled up on the couch watching a movie, or with both women on their knees at my feet—you never know. So what's hard isn't money, or even time; I'm thankful to have plenty of those, and we take at least three major vacations a year. One of my favorite things to do is stroll through an airport on our way to some lush beach locale, an arm wrapped possessively around each of the women. I make it clear that we are not mere traveling companions, but lovers, not with obnoxious public displays of affection, but by the simple yet powerful use of body language. All it takes is a hand lightly teasing Tanya's ass or a brush of Wendy's lips against my cheek to display to one and all what kind of vacation this will be. Showing off my beauties is a thrill I never take for granted, and it makes even the mundane task of going through airport security an opportunity for a little bit of exhibitionism.

In some ways, my two submissive, sexy sluts are a study in contrasts. Tanya is short and curvy, with natural red hair and freckles, while Wendy is almost as tall as I am (six feet), pale with jet-black hair. Next to them I tend to look rather middle of the road, but I don't mind; it just attracts more curiosity and attention once people realize that both women belong to me. I like to make people wonder what it is I've done to garner such female devotion; those who truly want to know are welcome to find out.

I've told them they're allowed to dress in jeans and sneakers when we travel, but they both have enough fashionista and exhibitionist in them to want to dress to the nines while in the air.

"After all, if you're gonna go, don't you want to look fabulous while doing it?" Tanya once joked, masking what I knew was a true fear of death by plane crash. That's another thing I love about her: she is relentlessly optimistic, and forces that optimism to override her fears, something she's applied to our BDSM play as well as all areas of her life. She teaches me just as much as I've taught her, and now that Wendy is a part of our lives, I see Tanya teaching Wendy what it truly means to submit, while I oversee their erotic education.

I've learned so much about women from living with two of them, seeing how they are different and how they are alike, how they behave similarly when surrendering to me, and differently. Yes, Wendy is our slave, but she's as much a part of our family as anyone else; both Tanya and I would take a bullet for her. Her slave status is not a trapping; rather, it's a way of life, a way of relating that makes life richer for all of us. They are both extremely eager to please, to provide, to obey, but each does so in slightly different ways. I know exactly how hard each of them can be pushed, what kinds of spankings they can take, how much they like to struggle, what naughty words push them to the edge of orgasm. It's this ongoing process of learning, of plotting what will thrill each of them, that makes being their master a joy and, at times, a challenge, one I willingly take on with pride.

I've encountered plenty of men who've looked over at my darling Wendy, bejeweled with hoops through each nipple and one through her clit, her gleaming black hair glistening down her back, the collar around her neck, being led around by my wife, Tanya, or tethered to me, and hinted that I must be the luckiest man alive. "A gorgeous wife and a stunning slave who'll do whatever you want? Two women completely at your bidding? You have it made, man." They're right, and yet not for the reasons they think.

I take owning Wendy very seriously, as does Tanya, and the truth is if it were just me, I don't think I'd want the weight of responsibility caring for Wendy brings. Of course she's utterly gorgeous, with her sensuous body, curves in all the right places, a beautiful face, and an endless appetite for sex, humiliation and beatings. In fact, her appetite, I daresay, exceeds mine, and mine is pretty healthy. That's why sharing her with Tanya works perfectly. I knew when I married Tanya that if I didn't want to lose her to a woman, I'd have to find a way to bring a woman to her; she'd told me as much when I proposed. And as I stated already, Wendy brings in her fair share of money, but it is a challenging relationship; she is constantly pushing both of us further in this dance of dominance and submission, and she brings out a side of me that even Tanya doesn't always. I wouldn't admit it to her, but there are moments when our exquisite exchanges stun me, awe me—scare me, even. They are so raw, so far from the trappings of collars and clamps, going straight to the heart of what makes us human.

That is why sharing Wendy works so perfectly, giving both Tanya and me a chance to unleash all that power that coils inside us, unfurling it onto the most willing of women, for whom "victim" has never been a word in her personal vocabulary. There's something achingly beautiful about the way Wendy stares straight at me—when she's not blindfolded, that is—as I strike her, as I pour candle wax onto her, as I engage in all manner of torments. She likes to watch and anticipate.

We met Wendy at a party where a man had been halfheartedly flinging a flogger at her beautiful breasts, hardly even looking where it landed, certainly not noticing the disappointment she couldn't quite keep off her face that his swats weren't quite firm or sadistic enough. I reached beneath Tanya's flimsy slip and pinched her nipples, twisting them until I felt the rest of her body writhe in recognition and desire. "I think you should go over there and show that man how it's done," I whispered. I love watching Tanya control another woman; she's more sub than top, but on the occasions when she does top, it brings out a fierceness that makes her seem much taller than five foot four, and I know it feeds something in her soul, just as being rough with her feeds something in mine.

For the most part, I top both Tanya and Wendy separately, though occasionally at the same time; if you think having one woman on her knees, naked, hands shackled behind her back, staring up at you with utter adoration, desire and need is hot, try having two of them. But every once in a while, Tanya gets the urge to let her domme side out; it happens seemingly at random, and I don't question it. She is statuesque and beautiful, and can work a whip, not to mention her voice, like the most professional of dominatrices. Seeing her wield that power on Wendy is indescribably exquisite, though I'll try. It's like I get to see a side of her that's just for me—and Wendy. I know that Tanya knows exactly what she's doing, every step of the way, and I take pride in watching her.

Joining her is a whole other level of thrill ride. When we co-top, the energy flows from me to Tanya to Wendy and back, an endless loop of sexual power and pleasure that makes me feel electrified. Another reason to like a little spark in your submissives? They manage to keep you on your toes, and surprise you with their penchant for creative kink, giving and taking in the most glorious ways. I wouldn't trade Tanya for a girl who always said "yes" if my life depended on it, because what I get in exchange for her bursts of riotous color is priceless.

For my birthday last week, Tanya took things to a whole new level, surprising me in a huge way. We'd recently redecorated our entire house, and she'd purchased a custom-made bit of furniture, without my being any the wiser. Again, one of the bonuses of marrying a smart woman is that she's able to pull off tricks like hiring a custom woodworker to make a St. Andrew's cross, one fitted perfectly to either Wendy's or Tanya's size. She'd even found a woman to do the job, and had invited her for its unveiling—with Wendy strapped right in. Daphne didn't look like a woman who worked with her hands, until you got up close. Instead, she looked like she didn't work at all, but rather, oversaw other people's work; even her smile had a commanding air, her teeth gleaming perfectly white, her lipstick ultra red.

"Honey, after dinner, I want to give you your present," Tanya had said to me as we dined at our favorite Italian restaurant. Tanya had picked at her food, which I found odd, since I know what an appetite she has, and I love watching her eat, but I'd been more than happy to guess what the gift was, though I didn't come close at all.

After I'd guessed vacation, new bespoke suit, even a car, she leaned over the table, allowing me and anyone else watching a very generous glimpse of her cleavage, and kissed me on the lips. "No more guesses; you'll just have to trust me." She raised her eyebrows at me; that's what I've told her countless times during our marriage when I knew she'd wind up enjoying some sadistic act I'd cooked up but she was hesitant. And of course, she was right.

I even let her blindfold me for the very first time and lead me down the stairs, where I could hear Wendy making little moaning noises that instantly made me hard. I was thinking that maybe she had Wendy naked and dressed up just for me, which she did, but Wendy wasn't just adorned—she was kneeling with her legs spread in front of my birthday gift, every part of her open, exposed, waiting for me—and my wife. The sight alone could have made me come, but I wouldn't let myself climax without first fully enjoying what my women had to offer me.

Not only was Tanya at her fiercest, but we had an audience, something we'd never had before. Wendy looked perfect, dolled up for the occasion. Yes, even a naked girl can make an effort. She was on her knees, head tilted slightly back so her breasts stood up proudly. Wendy wore thick black cuffs around her wrists. Her large nipples protruded—and glittered. The effect was subtle but gorgeous, a perfect complement to the twin silver hoops through each pink, beautiful nub. Her pussy was bare, and so open, as if just waiting for us to attack it. Her long silky hair hung down her back, and while her face was bare save for some gloss, it too wore something that money couldn't buy—bliss.

She was excited, that much was clear. Tanya beckoned me over with a cat-that-ate-the-canary smile. "Isn't she perfect?" she asked, taking a feather and trailing it from our beloved's forehead, then down, detouring along her cheek, then her neck, then her armpit, nipple and belly. "Stand up, lean against the cross and spread your legs," Tanya ordered, before tracing the feather along Wendy's inner thighs, then wetting it between her legs. "She's all ready for us to play with, and I have some new toys. I know she's ready, too," she said, and took my hand to her lips, kissing my fingertips lightly, before guiding them to Wendy's waiting pussy. Our slave was soaking wet; she didn't make a sound as I lightly stroked her, but she didn't need to. Her pussy told me everything I needed to know. Tanya attached Wendy's wrist cuffs to the St. Andrew's cross.

"So what do you have planned for our beautiful slave?" I asked Tanya, making sure to step aside so Daphne could get a proper view. "We have to make sure our guest enjoys herself after giving us this contribution to our household, don't we?" I knew what I wanted to do—sink my entire hand into Wendy's wet, hungry pussy, then when I was done, watch Tanya do the same. Fisting wasn't something we did very often, which made it all the more exciting. But I wanted to let Tanya lead the show; she has just as sadistic and devious mind as I do. If I hadn't known that already, the toys she presented to me would've been proof enough. One was a gigantic black dildo with a flared base, almost monstrously large, easily twice the size of my cock, which isn't on the small side. There were two kinds of nipple clamps, a roll of duct tape, a butt plug and assorted cuffs, clamps and whips.

"How long have you been waiting for us, Wendy?" I asked, picking up the feather and tickling her cheek, then along her neck. She squirmed, making her breasts jiggle, but didn't answer me. I reached down and rested my fingers against her pussy, feeling Tanya's fingers join me as we both pressed her. "I think you'd better answer me," I growled, sliding my fingers out to pinch her clit.

"About an hour," she said, the words making her tremble. I moved my fingers and explored her inner thighs while Tanya smiled at me, then kissed Wendy forcefully before moving on to using her teeth, nipping her way along our slave's skin, from her neck on down. Part of me longed to simply watch Tanya leave bite marks on Wendy's inner arm, lipstick traces on her stomach, and then see her head buried between Wendy's legs, but I wanted to participate even more. I pulled open the velvet pouch containing Tanya's recent purchases and found a suede flogger in purple, Wendy's favorite color. Reaching deeper, I also unearthed a red ball gag.

"Honey," I asked when Tanya came up for air, "should we use this?" I held up the gag. "Or do you want to hear this pretty thing scream?" When Tanya didn't give me an answer right away, I deferred to Daphne. "Daphne, as our guest, maybe you can decide this important matter."

"I think her screams would sound lovely," she replied with a flirtatious lilt to her voice that left me wondering whether she most enjoyed being on the giving or receiving end of such screams.

"That decides it," I said, smiling at Wendy as I gave her cheek a light slap. She shuddered in response, and I stared deep into her eyes. Slapping her sweet face is one of the things I enjoy most. "If you're good, you might get more of those," I told her.

It was Tanya's turn to dig through her toy bag, and she came up with what I could tell was a small but powerful pink vibrator. "Can you hold this for a minute?" she asked, placing it in my hand, then lubing up the monster dildo before taking it back from me. My wife is incredibly dexterous, and I knew she could easily handle two toys at once—the question was, could Wendy? Or rather, could Wendy handle the dildo, the vibrator and me flogging her? We were about to find out.

I was a gentleman—yes, even we sadists can be gentlemen—and allowed Tanya to go first. She started by pressing the head of the dildo against Wendy's wide-open pussy. It was so big that even though our slave was wet as could be, it would require a little effort on both their parts to get it inside. "I know you can take this, Wendy—I know you're going to take it, because if you can't, we're going to have to go across the room and torture Daphne instead of you, and that would be disappointing, wouldn't it?" Tanya used a voice that was partly teasing, partly coaxing, all vixen. It was a purr with an underlying edge that let Wendy know that to disappoint Tanya would be a very grave error. "That's better. Give us your pussy," Tanya said. "You know we own it anyway." She paused and pulled the toy out, making Wendy moan with disappointment, but my wife was back in a flash, now holding the vibrator against Wendy's clit while she manipulated the dildo against Wendy's wetness. The noise of the toys pressing against her and Wendy's soft moans made me rock hard. Tanya continued her stream of dirty talk. "I've seen Jack get his whole hand inside you, so I know this toy shouldn't be a problem. I even told the woman at the shop about you; I said that I wanted the biggest dildo they had in stock because I had a very greedy, horny slut slave at home waiting for me to fill her up all the way. I showed her your photo—"

At that, Wendy let out a cry, wriggling and sweating, her lipstick starting to fade from chewing on her lip as the dildo slipped all the way inside her under Tanya's artful grasp. My wife's tone immediately switched to a sweeter note; the woman definitely knew what she was doing. She smiled at us, a truly tender smile, and said, "That's it, baby, I always knew you were going to get this inside you. I know you can do anything you want to do, and anything that we want you to, because we own you, and we know what you're going to like. And you like the way that toy feels stretching out your pussy, don't you?" The garbled response was more than sufficient to let us know Wendy's answer. I was bursting with pride—and arousal. Tanya can somehow be tough as nails as a top but, standing so near her, I knew that if at that moment I grabbed the toys from her hands and demanded she be the one to spread her legs, she would do it for me in a heartbeat, not caring whether Wendy, or Daphne, saw her debased, degraded—and loving it. I was tempted, but they were both having too much fun.

Instead, I joined them, taking the flogger and hitting Wendy hard across her chest. Tanya ducked down, crouching at Wendy's feet in a beautifully servile position, to give me the space I needed to do justice to the flogging. The sounds of Wendy's moans, the flogger hitting her skin, and the toy whirring against her clit, along with her wetness as she responded to the dildo, was musical, magical. I placed my hand over Wendy's mouth for a moment, almost coming as I felt her lips try to twitch, the sounds trapped inside her as her body heated up along with our play. A quick glance over at Daphne found her rapt with attention, delighted at the live sex show she was, in a way, a part of. That gave me an idea. I curled my finger and beckoned Daphne over. I didn't know the woman at all, but that made it hotter. I took my hand off Wendy's mouth and placed the handle of the flogger between her lips. "Don't let that fall," I barked.

She whimpered, but nodded. "Enjoying yourself, Daphne?" I asked, noticing her hard nipples beneath her off-white blouse; I love when women who definitely need bras don't wear them.

"Yes," she said breathlessly.

"I can tell," I said, then chanced reaching out and taking one nipple between my fingers. She cried out, but kept eye contact. I did the same to the other one. "Do you want a turn up here—a chance to enjoy your own craftsmanship?" I twisted her nipples harder, then ripped open her blouse, one button falling to the floor as I grasped her buds directly. I pinched them hard, twisting, waiting for her answer. We were playing a new kind of game, one where the longer she took to respond, the more I tortured her nipples.

"You better answer me, or I'm not going to give you a choice." Her breath hitched and she melted into my hands, letting me know she wanted what I was about to do next. I took her breast and lifted it toward my mouth, then bit hard, satisfied at the gasp I heard.

"Tanya, take out the dildo from our pretty plaything, get Wendy down and tie her to that chair right there. Make sure her legs are spread wide open so I can see how wet she is for me, because after we're done with Daphne I want to fuck this sweet pussy of ours." Before turning Wendy over to Tanya, I myself removed the flogger from between her lips; maybe it was my imagination, but the O her mouth formed when I did seemed to beg to be filled again—but I had better things to do at the moment.

Tanya didn't question me, just gave me a sexy smile as I pulled Daphne close for a kiss. Her body surrendered to me, relaxing in my arms, letting me claim it with each press of my fingers against her ass, each thrust of my tongue into her mouth. I rarely take another woman, since I have my hands—and other body parts—full, but when one as pliable and hungry as Daphne enters my realm, I can't help myself.

In seemingly no time, Wendy, a look of pure submissive bliss on her face, was being led to the chair by Tanya, while I secured a trembling, beautiful Daphne into the bonds of the cross. Some people feel truly at one, at peace, when they reach the top of a mountain peak or run a marathon or eat the juiciest, ripest peach. We all take our bliss where we can, and I take mine in the act—or rather, acts—of bringing a woman from free to claimed, from untethered to bound, from autonomous to owned. It can last for a minute or an hour or forever, but it's that process of transferring power, energy, need, of claiming my willing captive, that makes me come alive, especially with a woman who experiences a corresponding rapture when I do. Daphne practically purred as I strapped her in. I thought about getting her naked first, but it was more fun to let her wrinkled blouse fall open, bunch her skirt around her hips and rip apart her flimsy panties with my hands. A woman can be just as naked in dishabille as she can in the buff.

I glanced over and found Wendy looking at one with the chair; Tanya is a quick study when it comes to rope, and she was just finishing securing our slave's wrists behind her back. Even though several feet separated us, I felt so in tune with my wife, so in sync as we each set about preparing the waiting women before us for their masochistic dream come true. I didn't know what Daphne was used to when it came to playing, but clearly a woman who could manufacture furniture like a St. Andrew's cross knew a thing or two about what she had just stepped into. I heard a smack, and resisted staring too long as Tanya slapped Wendy's face, then her nipples, with her hand. I turned to Daphne and fed her my fingers, her instantaneous sucking making me long for those lips to be wrapped around my dick, but there'd be another time for that, I was sure of it. Sometimes a good master has to forgo the immediacy of sexual pleasure in favor of another kind of pleasure entirely, that of ownership, command, control. Seeing the look on Daphne's face when I pulled my fingers out of her mouth, the loss leaving her forlorn, gave me a different kind of pride.

"Don't worry, sweetheart, I'll keep your mouth busy," I said to her, then replaced my fingers with the tan dildo I'd just grabbed from the bag. It was on the small side, but that didn't matter. This was about possession, not size, and watching Daphne's lips open automatically as I shoved it deep into her throat was beautiful. I took one last glance behind me and found Tanya straddling Wendy's leg, grinding against her thigh with her naked pussy as she ran a Wartenburg wheel along our slave's skin, just above her nipple.

"You could probably fit two cocks in that pretty mouth, couldn't you?" I asked Daphne, and she gurgled an attempt at a response around the invading dick. "Now I need my hands to beat you, so you keep that in your mouth like a good girl." I found a small strap that would be perfect on her front. I tried it out on my hand, smiling at the sting it caused. Daphne's eyes smiled back at me in lieu of her mouth, which was too busy.

I added to the cacophony in the room now that Tanya had moved on to slapping Wendy's bare thighs and making her count the slaps, as I struck Daphne with hard, pointed strikes of the leather slapper. I made sure to alternate my blows—one to her upper arm, one to her cutely curved belly, one to the point of each nipple, then a light tap against her cheek, intended more to startle her than hurt—the sound making my dick unbearably hard. In barely any time at all, her pale skin was covered in light bruises I knew would continue to blossom once she left. I took the dildo out of her mouth and slid it between her legs, making her gasp. Because she liked it, I only gave her a little of the toy, my eyes drilling into hers, daring her to ask for more. She didn't squirm, didn't beg, but I could tell she was tightening her inner muscles around the dildo, trying to get as much satisfaction as she could.

"Is that what you're gonna do to my cock if I fuck you?" I asked, at the same moment shoving it all the way inside her. Daphne's body shuddered as she eked out a "Yes." I fucked her hard, until I felt her juices dripping down the toy and onto my hand. I used my other hand to manipulate her clit, going slower this time as I coaxed a second orgasm from her, while Wendy's cries of pleasure rang out in the room. When Daphne came again, I eased the toy out, then slipped it between her fingers; her wrists were bound, but she could still hold the wet toy, feel her wetness and be reminded of what she'd just done.

"You're going to stay up there now and watch me and Tanya, and if you're good and quiet, maybe next time you'll be the one getting fucked. Tanya, get over here," I said, and like the perfect wife she is, Tanya paused right after her last smack; by this point, she had untied Wendy and had her bent over the chair. I heard her whisper, "Stay there," as she crawled over to me. Knowing Daphne and Wendy were watching Tanya make her way across the room added to my arousal.

I whipped out my dick, holding the base in my hand as Tanya

reached me and immediately began sucking, hands resting behind her back. I resisted the temptation to grab her hair and shove her closer, but I liked seeing her struggle to take all of me, to balance, to perform. Taking her, using her, after she's just released her top energy upon another gorgeous woman is the absolute apotheosis of kinky delight for me, like she's come full circle, come home. I didn't have to tell the other women to watch and learn; without even looking, I knew their eyes were glued on us, and when I was ready, I finally did take Tanya's soft red hair in my hand, holding her back, staring down into her beautiful face as I painted it with my come. "Now go give our girls a kiss," I said, "so they know what I taste like." She did exactly as I said, until all three of them had beautifully smeared smiles on their faces. I smiled back at each of them. Mastering two women—or, in this case, three—may not be the easiest job in the world, but it's certainly the best one I've ever held.

ABOUT THE AUTHORS

LAURA ANTONIOU (LAntoniou.com) has been writing erotica for over twenty years. Best known for her Marketplace series, she has also lectured at over one hundred events worldwide. Her most recent novel, *The Killer Wore Leather*, is a comedy/murder mystery set within the leather/BDSM world.

MICHELLE AUGELLO-PAGE (michelleaugellopage.wordpress.com) writes poetry, erotica and dark fiction. Her work has appeared in art galleries, online journals, print publications, anthologies, audio and e-book formats. Her erotic stories have been published in the Cleis Press anthologies *Fairy Tale Lust*, *Lustfully Ever After* and *Duty and Desire*.

EMILY BINGHAM is a Portland, Oregon, author whose writing has appeared in *Best Bondage Erotica 2011, Serving Him: Sexy Stories of Submission* and on Cleansheets.com. She is a leg wear and fetish model for photographers across the country.

Her adventures in rope can be found at her erotic writing blog queanofrope.com.

JACQUELINE BROCKER (jacquelinebrocker.esquinx.net) is an Australian writer living in the U.K. Her short erotic fiction has appeared in *My First Spanking*, *The Mammoth Book of Quick and Dirty Erotica* and *Under Her Thumb* (Cleis Press). Her novella *Body & Bow* was published by Forbidden Fiction.

ELIZABETH COLDWELL (elizabethcoldwell.wordpress. com) lives and writes in London. Her stories have appeared in numerous anthologies, including *Best Bondage Erotica 2011, 2012* and *2013*.

ROXANNA CROSS is the emerging voice to heat up sex lives of readers everywhere—she *really* enjoys discovering new and kinky ways to spice up her marital bed.

KATHLEEN DELANEY-ADAMS is a stone high femme porn writer and spoken word performer. A national touring veteran, Kathleen is the founder and producer of BODY HEAT: Femme Porn Tour, now in its seventh year. A submissive 1950s house-wife at heart, Kathleen's current writing project is a Year of Cupcakes, belovedcupcake.blogspot.com/.

LUCY FELTHOUSE (lucyfelthouse.co.uk) is a very busy woman! She writes erotica and erotic romance in a variety of subgenres and pairings, and has over seventy publications to her name, with many more in the pipeline. These include stories in *Best Bondage Erotica 2012* and *2013* and *Best Women's Erotica 2013*.

TILLY HUNTER (tillyhuntererotica.blogspot.co.uk) is a British author with a wicked imagination and a taste for quirky erotica. She has stories in the anthologies *Cherry Ripe* and *Miss Pemberton's Drawers*, *Smut Alfresco* and *Lust in Time*.

KAY JAYBEE (kayjaybee.me.uk) is the author of *The Voyeur*, (Xcite 2012), *Making Him Wait* (Sweetmeats, 2012), *The Perfect Submissive (*Xcite, 2011*)*, *A Sticky Situation* (Xcite 2012), *Yes, Ma'am* (Xcite, 2011), and *The Collector* (Austin & Macauley, 2012).

ANNABEL JOSEPH (annabeljoseph.com) is a multi-published kinky novelist whose stories celebrate the complexity and romance of erotic power exchange. When she's not penning hot BDSM tales, she's on Twitter discussing orgasm denial, trapeze sex and other such vital topics.

ANNABETH LEONG (annabethleong.blogspot.com) has often heard eels disparaged, but admires their spunk. Her stories have appeared in *Best Bondage Erotica 2013*, *Forever Bound*, and more than twenty other anthologies.

SOMMER MARSDEN (sommermarsden.blogspot.com) has been called "...one of the top storytellers in the erotica genre" (Violet Blue) and "Unapologetic" (Alison Tyler). Her erotic novels include *Boys Next Door, Learning to Drown* and *Restless Spirit*.

JAMES MCARTHUR is an author of kinky m/m erotica who loves tales of ordinary guys desperate to be tied up and the men who'll oblige. He lives in Britain and when he's not writing, he enjoys trail running and pottering in his allotment shed.

RAZIEL MOORE started writing erotic fiction in the late 1980s and cofounded The Erotic Writer blog (eroticwriter.wordpress.com) in 2009. He is published in several print anthologies, and a number of e-zines and e-books. Raziel lives in the Northeastern United States.

Erotica writer **GISELLE RENARDE** is a queer Canadian, avid volunteer, contributor to more than one hundred short story anthologies and author of numerous electronic and print books, including *Anonymous, Nanny State* and *My Mistress' Thighs*.

TERESA NOELLE ROBERTS (teresanoelleroberts.com) writes sexy stories for lusty romantics of all persuasions. Her work has appeared in *Best Bondage Erotica 2011, 2012* and *2013* and other provocatively titled anthologies. Look for BDSM romance *Knowing the Ropes* and the paranormal Duals and Donovans series from Samhain.

L. C. SPOERING (lcspoering.wordpress.com) is a Denver native and a graduate of the University of Colorado, with a BA in writing. Sharing her home with a husband, two kids and a plethora of pets, she writes novels and short stories about the human experience, relationships and the lives lived in between.

KISSA STARLING (kissastarling.com) is a multi-published author whose stories focus on characters' relationships regardless of genre or pairing. She's a member of Romance Divas, Midnight Seduction Authors and The Golden Crown Literary Society. Her work can be purchased at Red Rose Publishing, Cleis Press, Atria Books, Sapphire Publishing and Renaissance E-Books.

KATHLEEN TUDOR (KathleenTudor.com) is a rockin' erotic author and super-editor, with stories in anthologies from Cleis, Circlet, Storm Moon, Mischief HarperCollins, Circlet, Xcite and more. Check her out in *Take Me, My Boyfriend's Boyfriends* and *Kiss Me at Midnight.*

ABOUT THE EDITOR

RACHEL KRAMER BUSSEL (rachelkramerbussel.com) is an author, editor and blogger. She has edited over fifty books of erotica, including *The Big Book of Orgasms; Twice the Pleasure: Bisexual Women's Erotica; Serving Him: Sexy Stories of Submission; Anything for You; Suite Encounters; Going Down; Irresistible; Gotta Have It; Obsessed; Women in Lust; Surrender; Orgasmic; Cheeky Spanking Stories; Bottoms Up; Spanked: Red-Cheeked Erotica; The Mile High Club; Going Down; Tasting Him; Tasting Her; Please, Sir; Please, Ma'am; He's on Top; She's on Top; Lust in Latex* and is *Best Bondage Erotica* series editor. Her anthologies have won eight IPPY (Independent Publisher) Awards, and *Surrender* won the National Leather Association Samois Anthology Award. Her work has been published in over one hundred anthologies, including *Best American Erotica 2004* and *2006*. She wrote the popular "Lusty Lady" column for the *Village Voice*.

Rachel has written for *AVN, Bust,* Cleansheets.com, *Cosmo-*

politan, Curve, The Daily Beast, TheFrisky.com, *Glamour,* Gothamist, Huffington Post, *Inked,* Mediabistro, *Newsday, New York Post, New York Observer, Penthouse,* The Root, Salon, *San Francisco Chronicle, Time Out New York* and *Zink,* among others. She has appeared on "The Gayle King Show," "The Martha Stewart Show," "The Berman and Berman Show," NY1 and Showtime's "Family Business." She teaches erotic writing workshops across the country at colleges, sex toy stores, conferences and community events. She blogs at lustylady.blogspot.com and Tweets @raquelita.

More from Rachel Kramer Bussel

Do Not Disturb
Hotel Sex Stories
Edited by Rachel Kramer Bussel

A delicious array of hotel hookups where it seems like any-thing can happen—and quite often does. "If *Do Not Disturb* were a hotel, it would be a 5-star hotel with the luxury of 24/7 entertainment available."—Erotica Revealed
978-1-57344-344-9 $14.95

Bottoms Up
Spanking Good Stories
Edited by Rachel Kramer Bussel

As sweet as it is kinky, *Bottoms Up* will propel you to pick up a paddle and share in both pleasure and pain, or perhaps simply turn the other cheek.
ISBN 978-1-57344-362-3 $15.95

Orgasmic
Erotica for Women
Edited by Rachel Kramer Bussel

What gets you off ? Let *Orgasmic* count the ways...with 25 stories focused on female orgasm, there is something here for every reader.
ISBN 978-1-57344-402-6 $14.95

Please, Sir
Erotic Stories of Female Submission
Edited by Rachel Kramer Bussel

These 22 kinky stories celebrate the thrill of submission by women who know exactly what they want.
ISBN 978-1-57344-389-0 $14.95

Fast Girls
Erotica for Women
Edited by Rachel Kramer Bussel

Fast Girls celebrates the girl with a reputation, the girl who goes all the way, and the girl who doesn't know how to say "no."
ISBN 978-1-57344-384-5 $14.95

Many More Than Fifty Shades of Erotica

Please, Sir
Erotic Stories of Female Submission
Edited by Rachel Kramer Bussel

If you liked *Fifty Shades of Grey,* you'll love the explosive stories of *Please, Sir.* These damsels delight in the pleasures of taking risks to be rewarded by the men who know their deepest desires. Find out why nothing is as hot as the power of the words "Please, Sir."
ISBN 978-1-57344-389-0 $14.95

Yes, Sir
Erotic Stories of Female Submission
Edited by Rachel Kramer Bussel

Bound, gagged or spanked—or controlled with just a glance—these lucky women experience the breathtaking thrills of sexual submission. *Yes, Sir* shows that pleasure is best when dispensed by a firm hand.
ISBN 978-1-57344-310-4 $15.95

He's on Top
Erotic Stories of Male Dominance and Female Submission
Edited by Rachel Kramer Bussel

As true tops, the bossy hunks in these stories understand that BDSM is about exulting in power that is freely yielded. These kinky stories celebrate women who know exactly what they want.
ISBN 978-1-57344-270-1 $14.95

Best Bondage Erotica 2013
Edited by Rachel Kramer Bussel

Let *Best Bondage Erotica 2013* be your kinky playbook to erotic restraint—from silk ties and rope to shiny cuffs, blindfolds and so much more. These stories of forbidden desire will captivate, shock and arouse you.
ISBN 978-1-57344-897-0 $15.95

Luscious
Stories of Anal Eroticism
Edited by Alison Tyler

Discover all the erotic possibilities that exist between the sheets and between the cheeks in this daring collection. "Alison Tyler is an author to rely on for steamy, sexy page turners! Try her!"—Powell's Books
ISBN 978-1-57344-760-7 $15.95

Happy Endings Forever And Ever

Buy 4 books, Get 1 FREE*

Dark Secret Love
A Story of Submission
By Alison Tyler

Inspired by her own BDSM exploits and private diaries, Alison Tyler draws on twenty-five years of penning sultry stories to create a scorchingly hot work of fiction, a memoir-inspired novel with reality at its core. A modern-day *Story of O*, a *9 1/2 Weeks*-style journey fueled by lust, longing and the search for true love.
ISBN 978-1-57344-956-4 $16.95

High-Octane Heroes
Erotic Romance for Women
Edited by Delilah Devlin

One glance and your heart will melt—these chiseled, brave men will ignite your fantasies with their courage and charisma. Award-winning romance writer Delilah Devlin has gathered stories of hunky, red-blooded guys who enter danger zones in the name of duty, honor, country and even love.
ISBN 978-1-57344-969-4 $15.95

Duty and Desire
Military Erotic Romance
Edited by Kristina Wright

The only thing stronger than the call of duty is the call of desire. *Duty and Desire* enlists a team of hot-blooded men and women from every branch of the military who serve their country and follow their hearts.
ISBN 978-1-57344-823-9 $15.95

Smokin' Hot Firemen
Erotic Romance Stories for Women
Edited by Delilah Devlin

Delilah delivers tales of these courageous men breaking down doors to steal readers' hearts! *Smokin' Hot Firemen* imagines the romantic possibilities of being held against a massively muscled chest by a man whose mission is to save lives and serve *every* need.
ISBN 978-1-57344-934-2 $15.95

Only You
Erotic Romance for Women
Edited by Rachel Kramer Bussel

Only You is full of tenderness, raw passion, love, longing and the many emotions that kindle true romance. The couples in *Only You* test the boundaries of their love to make their relationships stronger.
ISBN 978-1-57344-909-0 $15.95

Unleash Your Favorite Fantasies

The Big Book of Bondage
Sexy Tales of Erotic Restraint
Edited by Alison Tyler

Nobody likes bondage more than editrix Alison Tyler, who is
fascinated with the ecstasies of giving up, giving in, and en-
trusting one's pleasure (and pain) into the hands of another.
Delve into a world of unrestrained passion, where heart-stop-
ping dynamics will thrill and inspire you.
ISBN 978-1-57344-907-6 $15.95

Hurts So Good
Unrestrained Erotica
Edited by Alison Tyler
Intricately secured by ropes, locked in
handcuffs or bound simply by a lover's
command, the characters of *Hurts So Good*
find themselves in the throes of pleasurable
restraint in this indispensible collection by
prolific, award-winning editor Alison Tyler.
ISBN 978-1-57344-723-2 $14.95

Caught Looking
*Erotic Tales of Voyeurs and
Exhibitionists*
Edited by Alison Tyler
and Rachel Kramer Bussel

These scintillating fantasies take the reader
inside a world where people get to show
off, watch, and feel the vicarious thrill of
sex times two, their erotic power multiplied
by the eyes of another.
ISBN 978-1-57344-256-5 $14.95

Hide and Seek
*Erotic Tales of Voyeurs and
Exhibitionists*
Edited by Rachel Kramer Bussel
and Alison Tyler

Whether putting on a deliberate show
for an eager audience or peeking into the
hidden sex lives of their neighbors, these
show-offs and shy types go all out in their
quest for the perfect peep show.
ISBN 978-1-57344-419-4 $14.95

One Night Only
Erotic Encounters
Edited by Violet Blue

"Passion and lust play by different rules in
One Night Only. These are stories about
what happens when we have just that one
opportunity to ask for what we want—and
we take it… Enjoy the adventure."
—Violet Blue
ISBN 978-1-57344-756-0 $14.95

Red Hot Erotic Romance

Obsessed
Erotic Romance for Women
Edited by Rachel Kramer Bussel

These stories sizzle with the kind of obsession that is fueled by our deepest desires, the ones that hold couples together, the ones that haunt us and don't let go. Whether just-blooming passions, rekindled sparks or reinvented relationships, these lovers put the object of their obsession first.
ISBN 978-1-57344-718-8 $14.95

Passion
Erotic Romance for Women
Edited by Rachel Kramer Bussel

Love and sex have always been intimately intertwined—and *Passion* shows just how delicious the possibilities are when they mingle in this sensual collection edited by award-winning author Rachel Kramer Bussel.
ISBN 978-1-57344-415-6 $14.95

Girls Who Bite
Lesbian Vampire Erotica
Edited by Delilah Devlin

Bestselling romance writer Delilah Devlin and her contributors add fresh girl-on-girl blood to the pantheon of the paranormal. The stories in *Girls Who Bite* are varied, un-expected, and soul-scorching.
ISBN 978-1-57344-715-7 $14.95

Irresistible
Erotic Romance for Couples
Edited by Rachel Kramer Bussel

This prolific editor has gathered the most popular fantasies and created a sizzling, no-holds-barred collection of explicit encounters in which couples turn their deepest desires into reality.
978-1-57344-762-1 $14.95

Heat Wave
Hot, Hot, Hot Erotica
Edited by Alison Tyler

What could be sexier or more seductive than bare, sun-warmed skin? Bestselling erotica author Alison Tyler gathers explicit stories of summer sex bursting with the sweet eroticism of swimsuits, sprinklers and ripe strawberries.
ISBN 978-1-57344-710-2 $15.95

Fuel Your Fantasies

Carnal Machines
Steampunk Erotica
Edited by D. L. King

In this decadent fusing of technology and romance, outstanding contemporary erotica writers use the enthralling possibilities of the 19th-century steam age to tease and titillate.
ISBN 978-1-57344-654-9 $14.95

The Sweetest Kiss
Ravishing Vampire Erotica
Edited by D. L. King

These sanguine tales give new meaning to the term "dead sexy" and feature beautiful bloodsuckers whose desires go far beyond blood.
ISBN 978-1-57344-371-5 $15.95

The Handsome Prince
Gay Erotic Romance
Edited by Neil Plakcy

A bawdy collection of bedtime stories brimming with classic fairy tale characters, reimagined and recast for any man who has dreamt of the day his prince will come. These sexy stories fuel fantasies and remind us all of the power of true romance.
ISBN 978-1-57344-659-4 $14.95

Daughters of Darkness
Lesbian Vampire Tales
Edited by Pam Keesey

"A tribute to the sexually aggressive woman and her archetypal roles, from nurturing goddess to dangerous predator."
—*The Advocate*
ISBN 978-1-57344-233-6 $14.95

Dark Angels
Lesbian Vampire Erotica
Edited by Pam Keesey

Dark Angels collects tales of lesbian vampires, the quintessential bad girls, archetypes of passion and terror. These tales of desire are so sharply erotic you'll swear you've been bitten!
ISBN 978-1-57344-252-7 $13.95

Out of This World Romance

Steamlust
Steampunk Erotic Romance
Edited by Kristina Wright

Shiny brass and crushed velvet; mechanical inventions and romantic conventions; sexual fantasy and kinky fetish: this is a lush and fantastical world of women-centered stories and romantic scenarios, a first for steampunk fiction.
ISBN 978-1-57344-721-8 $14.95

The Sweetest Kiss
Ravishing Vampire Erotica
Edited by D. L. King

These sanguine tales give new meaning to the term "dead sexy" and feature beautiful bloodsuckers whose desires go far beyond blood.
ISBN 978-1-57344-371-5 $15.95

Dream Lover
Paranormal Tales of Erotic Romance
Edited by Kristina Wright

A potent potion of fun and sexy tales filled with male fairies and clairvoyant scientists, as well as darkly erotic tales of ghosts, shapeshifters and possession.
ISBN 978-1-57344-655-6 $14.95

Fairy Tale Lust
Erotic Fantasies for Women
Edited by Kristina Wright

Award-winning novelist and erotica writer Kristina Wright goes over the river and through the woods to find the sexiest fairy tales ever written.
ISBN 978-1-57344-397-5 $14.95

In Sleeping Beauty's Bed
Erotic Fairy Tales
By Mitzi Szereto

"Who can resist the erotic origins of fairy tales from Little Red to Rapunzel's long braid? Szereto knows her way around the mythic scholarship and the most outrageous sexual deviations in Pandora's Box."
—Susie Bright
ISBN 978-1-57344-367-8 $16.95

Best Erotica Series

"Gets racier every year."—*San Francisco Bay Guardian*

Best Women's Erotica 2013
Edited by Violet Blue
ISBN 978-1-57344-898-7 $15.95

Best Women's Erotica 2012
Edited by Violet Blue
ISBN 978-1-57344-755-3 $15.95

Best Women's Erotica 2011
Edited by Violet Blue
ISBN 978-1-57344-423-1 $15.95

Best Bondage Erotica 2013
Edited by Rachel Kramer Bussel
ISBN 978-1-57344-897-0 $15.95

Best Bondage Erotica 2012
Edited by Rachel Kramer Bussel
ISBN 978-1-57344-754-6 $15.95

Best Bondage Erotica 2011
Edited by Rachel Kramer Bussel
ISBN 978-1-57344-426-2 $15.95

Best Lesbian Erotica 2013
Edited by Kathleen Warnock.
Selected and introduced by
Jewelle Gomez.
ISBN 978-1-57344-896-3 $15.95

Best Lesbian Erotica 2012
Edited by Kathleen Warnock.
Selected and introduced by
Sinclair Sexsmith.
ISBN 978-1-57344-752-2 $15.95

Best Lesbian Erotica 2011
Edited by Kathleen Warnock.
Selected and introduced by Lea DeLaria.
ISBN 978-1-57344-425-5 $15.95

Best Gay Erotica 2013
Edited by Richard Labonté.
Selected and introduced by Paul Russell.
ISBN 978-1-57344-895-6 $15.95

Best Gay Erotica 2012
Edited by Richard Labonté.
Selected and introduced by
Larry Duplechan.
ISBN 978-1-57344-753-9 $15.95

Best Gay Erotica 2011
Edited by Richard Labonté.
Selected and introduced by
Kevin Killian.
ISBN 978-1-57344-424-8 $15.95

Best Fetish Erotica
Edited by Cara Bruce
ISBN 978-1-57344-355-5 $15.95

Best Bisexual Women's Erotica
Edited by Cara Bruce
ISBN 978-1-57344-320-3 $15.95

Best Lesbian Bondage Erotica
Edited by Tristan Taormino
ISBN 978-1-57344-287-9 $16.95

★ **Free book of equal or lesser value. Shipping and applicable sales tax extra.**
Cleis Press • (800) 780-2279 • orders@cleispress.com
www.cleispress.com

Ordering is easy! Call us toll free or fax us to place your MC/VISA order.
You can also mail the order form below with payment to:
Cleis Press, 2246 Sixth St., Berkeley, CA 94710.

ORDER FORM

QTY	TITLE	PRICE
____	_____	_____
____	_____	_____
____	_____	_____
____	_____	_____
____	_____	_____
____	_____	_____
____	_____	_____
____	_____	_____

SUBTOTAL _____

SHIPPING _____

SALES TAX _____

TOTAL _____

Add $3.95 postage/handling for the first book ordered and $1.00 for each additional book. Outside North America, please contact us for shipping rates. California residents add 9% sales tax. Payment in U.S. dollars only.

* Free book of equal or lesser value. Shipping and applicable sales tax extra.

Cleis Press • Phone: (800) 780-2279 • Fax: (510) 845-8001
orders@cleispress.com • www.cleispress.com
You'll find more great books on our website

Follow us on Twitter @cleispress • Friend/fan us on Facebook